PENGUIN BOOKS

THE WILD CHERRY TREE

Born in 1905, H. E. Bates was educated at Kettering Grammar School and worked as a journalist before publishing his first book, *The Two Sisters*, when he was twenty. In the next fifteen years he won a distinguished reputation for his stories about English country life. In 1941, as 'Flying Officer X', he wrote his two famous books of short stories – *The Greatest People in the World* and *How Sleep the Brave* – which were followed in 1944 by *Fair Stood the Wind for France*. These, and his subsequent novels of Burma, *The Purple Plain* and *The Jacaranda Tree*, and of India, *The Scarlet Sword*, stemming directly or indirectly from his war experience in the East, won him a new reputation and, apart from their success in Britain and America, have been translated into sixteen foreign languages. His writing took a new direction with the appearance in 1958 of *The Darling Buds of May*, the first of the popular Larkin family novels, which was followed by *A Breath of French Air*, *When the Green Woods Laugh*, and *Oh! To be in England* (1963). *A Lover's Flowers* (1971) is his most recent book.

H. E. BATES

The Wild Cherry Tree

PENGUIN BOOKS

Penguin Books Ltd, Harmondsworth, Middlesex, England
Penguin Books Australia Ltd, Ringwood, Victoria, Australia

—

First published in Great Britain by Michael Joseph 1968
Published in Penguin Books 1971

—

Copyright © Evensford Productions Ltd, 1968

—

Made and printed in Great Britain
by Hazell Watson & Viney Ltd,
Aylesbury, Bucks
Set in Linotype Pilgrim

Contents

Halibut Jones

HALIBUT JONES lay stretched at full length on top of a dry ditch, staring through the breathless August air at great sprays of blackberries gleaming on the hedgerow above. It had been a very good season for blackberries, a very hot season, and some of the berries were as fat and bloomed as grapes.

Very high up for gathering, though, Halibut thought, too high to reach without a good long hook. Everything had grown so tall and lush in the long hot summer, after the heavy rains of spring. You couldn't have it all ways, of course. What was good for one thing was bad for another. It was very bad for mushrooms. You had to go traipsing a long way to find a button or two : hardly worth the candle. It was very bad for fishing too. You couldn't find the worms and the elderberries were hardly ready yet. The rivers needed a good long flush-out before anything would come on the feed and you didn't even get much with night-lines.

Halibut had legs and a rump like a cart horse. He was tall with it too, well over six feet, and his belly ballooned over his thick leather belt like a tight umbrella. His hands were toad-brown and vast. Each finger was like the crabby neck of a tortoise. His mouth was a big beery pouch, red and heavy but wearily loose, so that most of the time it was hardly ever shut.

By contrast his eyes, though big, were very soft. They were also very blue and as they held the blackberries in deep contemplation they had a gentle, dreamy air. It would, he thought, soon be dinner-time and the hand that rubbed a bead or two of sweat off his nose was slightly weary too. Altogether it was stifling weather for moving about very much.

A few years ago he would have been at the blackberries like a whippet at a hare. He would have been up at the first crack of light and not done till dark. But nowadays nobody wanted them. The shops turned them down; people wanted the cultivated sort. It was the same with mushrooms. It was all cultivated nowadays, or frozen, or tinned. You couldn't make yourself an honest bob or two like you used to do in the old days.

The thought of money made him remember Miss Parkinson. He had promised several times to clip Miss Parkinson's privet hedge but somehow or other something always kept cropping up. It was a bad time of year for clipping hedges anyway. It would be better in the autumn, when it was cooler, after a good rain or two.

Miss Parkinson lived alone in a big bay-windowed house of Edwardian brick with a vast garden of decaying fruit trees and untidy hedges of gigantic size. She was great at making elderberry wine and bottling fruit and preserves and lemon curd and drying flowers for winter. She felt, like Halibut, that things were not as they used to be. The synthetic curse of modern times lay thick on everything. There was everywhere a sad drift from Nature.

It slowly occurred to Halibut that Miss Parkinson might not think unkindly, perhaps, towards a pound or two of blackberries. He could at least try out the land. He might even talk her into the price of a tin of gentles and then, in the evening perhaps, nab a trout or two. It was hardly the weather for trout, he knew, but it might be worth a go.

Presently he got slowly to his feet and stood unsteadily swaying from side to side on the edge of the ditch, very much like a boxer rising from a heavy count. The sun blistered his eyes. For a moment or two he seemed about to relapse but finally he heaved on his belt, hitched up his trousers and started to walk down the lane.

It was only five minutes' walk to Miss Parkinson's big rambling house but in the heat of mid-morning it seemed like a mile. Once he was sorely tempted to have a breather by sitting on the brick coping of a narrow stone bridge that spanned the little river at the foot of the lane but he somehow managed to resist it and dragged himself on.

'Ah! Mr Jones. Spendid man. I'd absolutely given you up for lost. I was afraid you'd never come and see me again. I had the shears sharpened, you'll be glad to know. I trust everything's all right with you?'

Miss Parkinson tended to suck at her teeth. She was like a fat rosy apple fresh from the oven, all puffed and warm and juicy. Even in the heat she was wearing green corduroy breeches, with robust home-knitted stockings of a brown-cow shade. Her grey wispy hair stood out like tufts of untidy feathers from a large barley-coloured sunhat tied under her chin with a piece of picture cord.

Halibut wiped his brow with the back of his hand and gave something like a sigh. Miss Parkinson said she was positive the hedge had grown a good foot or more since his last promise to come and deal with it. At the mere mention of the hedge Halibut, his dreamy eyes wandering across the sun-baked untidiness of the garden, looked as if he'd swallowed something slightly distasteful.

'But anyway here you are. That's the main thing. I don't know how you feel but I had an idea one ought to be utterly ruthless with it. Cut it practically to ground level. What do you say?'

Halibut looked pained and dubious and scratched his head and said he'd had the screws. That's why he hadn't been near. It had played him up something chronic, like billy-o. In any case it wasn't the weather for hedge-cutting. It was too early yet and too dry. She didn't want to have the hedge die on her, did she?

'Die? But privet's utterly indestructible. You couldn't kill it with a flame gun.'

'You cut that now and it'll be dead afore the month's out. Never breathe.'

Miss Parkinson said she was sorry he thought it inadvisable but perhaps now that he was here he might do some other job? Such as cutting the thistles in the orchard? They stood there like so many soldiers.

'And spread all that seed?' Halibut said. 'You don't want that seed spread everywheres.'

No, he started to tell her now, what he'd really come about was blackberries. He knew where he could get some real corkers, beauties, big as grapes. Only he'd have to get himself a good long hook made. They were so high up the hedge.

'I'm not sure I can do with blackberries. It's elderberries I really want. I could do with masses.'

Ah! he told her, it was too early yet for elderberries. They would be another three weeks or more. He wiped his forehead again on the back of his hand and let his tongue run wearily across his lips. He didn't suppose by any chance she could do with a couple of trout? That's if he could get them.

'Oh! my dear man. How gorgeous if you could. I've got Miss Jordan coming to supper tomorrow and they would be the very thing. I put up some pots of a special gooseberry sauce last month and it would go with them marvellously.'

Nothing like the real home-made stuff, Halibut said. He wondered what was in some of the muck they sold nowadays. The bread was no cop, the bacon was as salt as old Harry and you couldn't tell what was in the jam. Turnips and clover seed, he shouldn't wonder. Yes: he was glad she kept on with the real old-fashioned stuff.

'Well, what about the trout? You really think you might?'

Well, there was a bit of a problem there. Fust, he was clean out of hooks and then he wasn't sure if his line was all that good. Then he'd have to get the gentles.

'Gentles? Oh! yes, you mean those awful maggots. I thought you caught trout on flies?'

'Not where I go. They're real maggot eaters up there. Run a nice weight too.'

Halibut gave a long, dry, harsh cough. It sounded very bad and as the cough went on his neck turned an alarming cockerel red. Miss Parkinson looked suddenly alarmed too and said the cough sounded really dreadful and was he sure he hadn't picked up some sort of bug?

'Just the dry weather. Allus gits me like this. Can't take it too hot.' He coughed harshly again and this time with a groan. 'Feel I'll fetch me heart up sometimes.'

It had been rather trying, the weather, in some ways, Miss Parkinson admitted. A good rain would freshen the air. Wouldn't he like a drink of some sort? A cup of tea? Or a good long lime-juice with plenty of ice?

'The tea,' Halibut said, 'would only make me hotter. Very nice of you –'

'Stupid of me. I know what I'll give you. Of course. I've started to brew a home-made beer. Oh! it's the proper thing. You buy a sort of do-it-yourself pack. Hops and everything. I find it rather good.'

Halibut started to say that he'd bet anything it was better than the bottled muck you got nowadays, considering the price you paid, but Miss Parkinson stopped him by urging him to sit down for a minute or two while she went to fetch the beer. She didn't care a bit for that cough of his.

With another groan Halibut agreed that perhaps it wasn't at all a bad idea and let his big horse-strong frame positively collapse into Miss Parkinson's wheelbarrow.

When she came back, five minutes later, carrying a big glass jug of beer and two glasses, the first thing she said was :

'Oh! Mr Jones, I've just remembered something. I'm always meaning to ask you. Why do they call you Halibut?'

'Real name's Albert. Couldn't say it properly when I was a kid. Would pronounce it Allibut.'

'How interesting. It sort of suits you.'

Miss Parkinson gave him a glass and filled it with beer and then poured out a glass for herself. Halibut thanked her and then held the glass up to the light and said he thought it looked very nice and clear. It had a fair head on it too.

'Oh! I really find it rather good. Say it as shouldn't. It's immensely refreshing.'

Halibut took a good long drink and said he rather thought so too. It was almost in the real old-fashioned class. His cough had gone completely now and he was able in clear tones to praise once again Miss Parkinson's great talent in going in for the good old honest stuff. You couldn't beat Nature.

'I'm sure you're right. It's what I call this synthetic curse that's got hold of everything. Actually, I now make practically everything I eat and drink. Butter, cheese, bread. Meat doesn't worry me. It's not worth eating. Oh! would you care for some bread and cheese? The bread's the real wholemeal.'

Halibut thanked her and said he really wouldn't mind if he did. While she had gone into the house again he took off his jacket and helped himself to another short tot of beer. With the jacket rolled up as a cushion he found it pretty comfortable in the barrow. The beer was pretty fair too and in any case it was no weather for moving about very much.

'I cut you off a good big crusty bit. Now *that* I will say is good. You'll not get a better chunk of bread anywhere. Do you prefer hard cheese or soft? I actually brought you a bit of both.'

Beer in one hand and bread and cheese in the other Halibut relaxed with a look of almost benign indifference as to the qualities of hard and soft cheese. They were both very good; she was right about the bread too and once again he told her warmly that you couldn't beat Nature.

'Coming back to the trout,' she said. 'It would be absolutely splendid if you could manage it. It would be a marvellous treat and I'll make it well worth your while.'

Well, Halibut said, he was coming to that. He really hadn't got the price of the hooks and the gentles. He hadn't been able to do much in the way of work lately because of the screws and one thing and another and he was wondering how she felt about the chances of a bit of dead horse?

'Dead horse? Oh! yes, I see. If it means getting the trout, of course. You'd work it off on the hedge, I suppose?'

Oh! yes, on the hedge. He'd work it off on the hedge. In no time. As soon as the weather got right for it.

'And you'd like what? How much, I mean?'

Well, Halibut said, looking at the beer with fresh and even

fonder appraisal, he thought the hedge would be about a three quid job. Especially if she wanted it cut so low.

'I see,' Miss Parkinson said. 'But you won't leave it too long, I hope. There's burning all the clippings to be done and so on. I'd like it all thoroughly cleaned up.'

Have to wait till it got damper and cooler, Halibut said. Been too many fires this summer, what with this new caper of burning the stubbles and all that. She didn't want the place a-fire, did she?

'Far from it. Oh! by the way, I don't know why I should think of it now, but you did say you might bring me pigeons. I saw a marvellous recipe for *pâté* that I wanted to try out. I did give you a little something for cartridges.'

Halibut looked at Miss Parkinson almost sadly. His dreamy blue eyes were not only apologetic but moist. No: he hadn't forgotten about the pigeons. But gospel truth, what with the screws and everything he hadn't been able to save enough for a new licence for the gun. Besides, there weren't all that lot of pigeons about now. The big shoots had thinned them out something cruel.

'What a pity. I hear it's a wonderful year for partridges, though.'

Well, she'd heard wrong then, Halibut told her. They'd died like flies in the wet spring. And what hadn't died in the spring had got roasted alive in the damn stubble fires.

'How wretched. I'm awfully fond of a good young partridge. They were splendid you brought me last year.'

It was a bit better for pheasants, though, Halibut suddenly told her, almost with cheerfulness. They got a bit better chance, being raised as chicks. Still, it wasn't a fat lot of good thinking about pheasants if he hadn't got a licence for the gun, any more than it was thinking about trout if he hadn't got the hooks. That was where a bit of dead horse would help. It would get him sort of started again.

'I know that Miss Jordan's positively crying out for someone to get her potatoes up. I could mention it to her tomorrow.'

One job at a time, Halibut said. He was fair rushed off his feet as it was. For one thing he'd promised to clean out a ditch for Miss McIntyre –

'You promised *who*? You promised to work for that old b-b-b-*biddy*! That Scotch so-and-so – that piece of old haggis!'

Well, you had to be fair, Halibut started to say.

'Fair, my foot. I'm – well, I must say I'm surprised, I'm shocked. I hadn't the faintest idea you ever worked for that whisky-guzzler.'

Well, you had to go where the money was, Halibut said. She'd raised him up from five to seven bob an hour –

'It's treason!' Miss Parkinson said. 'It's lower than kidnapping! It's downright treachery.'

Well, there it was. You couldn't very well look a gift horse in the mouth, could you?

'Her breath would probably strike you dead if you did!'

Halibut started to say that sometimes he felt proper sorry for the old bit. Blind as a bat and shaking all over. He hadn't the heart to let her down.

'She's sinister, that's what she is. She pretends she can't see but all the time her eyes are ten times as sharp as her ears and by George that's saying something.'

'Well, I don't know about that, but I'm prit near dead broke meself. She was going to pay me yesterday but she couldn't find her purse.'

'Typical mean trick! She buys you off and then can't find her purse. The plain fact is you probably never will see the colour of her money.'

Then he would be down the course. He never would get the ruddy hooks. Or the trout. That's if she still wanted them.

'Of course I still want them. Well, I suppose there's nothing for it but to match her offer. Seven shillings an hour – only two years ago it used to be three. I'll be dead broke too.'

Well, everybody had got to live, Halibut said. Everything was going up all the time. Grub, bacca, beer –

At the mention of beer Miss Parkinson seemed suddenly to

relent. Almost as if ashamed of her outburst and partly as if afraid that Halibut might think her mean she said she understood perfectly how it was. Hastily she poured out more beer and said:

'But you will try hard for the trout, won't you?'

'It's a thing you got to be very cunning about, this trout lark. Know what I mean? You don't want to git me nabbed, do you?'

Oh! no, no. She certainly didn't want to get him nabbed, Miss Parkinson said. That would be dreadful. She earnestly begged him to help himself to more beer while she went into the house to find her own purse.

While she had gone Halibut totted out the rest of the beer and finished up the last of the bread and cheese. It was going to be a stifling afternoon, he thought. There wouldn't be much on the feed yet awhile. Still it would give him all the more time to get the hooks and the gentles.

When Miss Parkinson finally came back she was carrying a brown paper bag.

'I thought you might care for a few apples. There are such masses this year. These are the Pearmains. I tucked the dead horse in with them too.'

Halibut slowly dragged himself out of the wheelbarrow, grunting deep thanks. He betted they'd taste like apples too. Not like some of the muck you got in shops nowadays. All colour and tasting like flannel.

'I refuse to eat them. It's the synthetic curse again, as I say. But thank Heaven there are still one or two of us who know the real thing.'

She looked at him almost fondly. She might have been about to call him a kindred spirit. Instead she said:

'Well, I shall keep my fingers crossed. What time do you think I might expect you? – that's if you have any luck.'

What time did she get up of a morning? Halibut said.

'Oh! six. Never later.'

That was it then, Halibut said. He'd be round at crack of dawn.

He walked slowly down the lane, carrying his jacket in one hand and the apples and the dead horse in the other. By the little river the shade of a row of alders was dark and deep and the air struck almost cold.

He lay down on the grass, by the waterside, his head on his folded jacket, and looked at the sky burning in bright blue scraps above the leaves. A ripple of water running over stones was the only sound to break the air. There was no doubt about it, he thought, as he closed his eyes, Miss Parkinson was right about Nature. There was nothing like Nature.

It was too hot for fishing, though. He'd have to give the trout a good few hours yet, prit near till dark, he thought. Or would they bite just as well in the morning?

Well, he'd have a bit of a kip in the meantime anyway. And then later perhaps, when it cooled off a bit, he might call and see Miss McIntyre.

She was always good for a bob or two. And you never knew, he might even get her up to seven bob an hour. It was always worth a try.

The Wild Cherry Tree

WHILE traffic on the six-track motorway scoured its passage across the valley, a procession of metallic beetles flashing chromium eyes by day and white hot feelers of light by night, the Boormans lived out their lives on a pig-farm, on the raw edge of a grey white crack, almost a culvert, in the chalk hills above. It was sometimes difficult to tell, especially in the short, mud-dark days of winter, who were the Boormans and who the pigs.

Difficult, that is, with one exception : Mrs Boorman.

Every morning, as she slopped out of the house into the mouldering filth of the pig-yard, always ahead by an hour or more of Boorman and their five lumbering sons, she looked in fact less like a pig than a shabby, straddling scarecrow. Big, mud-caked gum-boots concealed whatever shape her legs had. A long sack-cloth apron shrouded her body into a flatness that might have been masculine. A wide grey felt trilby, tied under her chin, with a black fraying woollen scarf, concealed completely the colour of her hair and shaded the entire area of her face so fully that the eyes had no colour at all. And as if she were actually afraid of revealing any part of herself that might have given away the fact that she was a woman she wore, winter and summer, a vast pair of old leather driving gloves, so dark with dirt and use that they might have been perennially soaked in pig dung.

In this disguise there was no saying how old she was. Except that she walked with a rapid, springing step she might have been an ancient hag, timeless and tough as an oak, out of some equally timeless saga of a lost and distant peasantry. She was in fact forty-five. Her sons, if not actually born all at once, in a litter, had come to her in such rapid succession and they now looked so much alike, in gross shabbiness, that they might in fact have been a litter. Life with pigs had made them pig-like, sleepy, slobbering carcasses wallowing their way about the stinking clutter of surrounding sties and shacks and yards.

At one time a thick triangular copse had covered part of the hillside. Now generation after generation of pigs had rootled it into a churned morass of mud and stumps that resembled more than anything else a battlefield strewn with the fat corpses of the slain.

There were seven or eight acres of this grotesque desolation, made still more desolate in spring-time by the stubborn survival of a single wild cherry tree, tall above the scores of stumpy hazels, its white-flowered branches like some graceful and point-less flag of surrender long since forgotten. There were never less than a hundred and fifty pigs rootling at the churned earth and of these Mrs Boorman constantly cherished and nurtured twenty-five or thirty of her own.

This constant brood was her second family, a means for the bestowal of unspoken affection and above all a means to money of her own. From litter after litter she chose some ailing piglet, the dillin, the odd-one-out, and cosseted it with warmth and tenderness and teated milk bottle until it gained strength and, in the fullness of time, bore litters of its own.

Regularly she drove an old Ford truck into market, a dozen porkers netted in the back, bargained a fair deal for them and then, for the rest of the day, went on the strangest shopping sprees with the greater part of the money.

As jackdaws are supposed to hoard objects of useless bril-liance and some women jewellery of equally useless beauty, Mrs Boorman hoarded clothes : not merely clothes consistent with her class or even clothes to wear or display, but clothes simply to hide and hoard, secretly. Nor were they ordinary clothes. With an infinite display of taste she bought everything from matching purple underwear to jumpers of dazzling gold, savage vermilion and tropical emerald, from dinner gowns of tulip sheen to fur wraps of silver mink, from hats of delicate sauciness to high-heeled shoes of exquisite elegance, all with jewellery, powder and perfume to match. Out of a life utterly deprived of colour she reached out with a sort of primitive thirst and snatched at things rich, expensive, dazzling.

All these, like a secretive squirrel, she took home and stored in a vast oak bedroom wardrobe, promptly locking it up and hanging the key, tied to a piece of string, round her neck.

Then, every night, after Boorman and the five pig-like sons had gone off on some lumbering spree of their own, beer-swilling, playing bingo or darts or scoffing fish and chips with girls at cinemas, she emerged from her sackcloth into her own world of elegant adventure. She first locked the doors of the house, then boiled a three gallon saucepan of water and carried it upstairs. The house had no bathroom but she filled a big galvanised bath with water, then stripped completely naked, stood in it and started to wash herself down.

Her long bare figure, untrammelled by sackcloth, gum-boots and flabby trilby, now stood free in remarkable revelation. Hard, incessant work had made her muscular but also supple and spare. Her breasts, with their rather large rose-brown nipples, were so graceful and firm-standing that they might have belonged to a woman twenty years younger.

Her skin, of a curious smoky olive shade, was clean and smooth, without a blemish. The hair that could never be seen under the squashy trilby except when windy days blew the hat an inch or two off her face, was a deep coffee brown, without a trace of grey.

But if all this was both startling and unexpected she showed, in her nakedness, a still more remarkable touch of revelation. The eyes were suddenly revealed as exceptional in colour : not of the same deep brown in harmony with her hair but a very pure, clear, limpid blue. This colour succeeded in giving to her entire face a look of extraordinary innocence curiously combined with guilt. It was almost as if she were ashamed of what she was doing while being sensuously and marvellously thrilled in doing it. She might have been taking part in a clandestine act of love with a lover perpetually kept in hiding by day and brought out every night to join her moment of furtive and miraculous wonder.

When she finally dressed she did so unhurriedly, tasting the successive stages of it languidly, savouring the whole affair as if relishing exotic food. In the earlier part of it all she would pause to caress and uplift her breasts with fingers that were revealed as exceptionally long and, thanks to the eternal protection of driving gloves, remarkably well kept. Before putting on a dress – she had a great taste for long ones of rather flowing design, wideskirted and sown with sequins – she spent a long time brushing her hair. When this was finished she spent an even longer time choosing the earrings, necklace and bracelets she would wear. And then finally the fur coat.

All this took her two hours or so. When she was finally ready it never appeared to disturb her, or to seem ridiculous, that she had no one to see her and nowhere to go. She had no desire to be seen, nor was there anywhere to go except into the sludge of the pig-yard.

Not, in fact, for many years: until at last, unaccountably attracted by an April evening of exceptional warmth after a day that had dried out even the pig-yard into a crust resembling brown concrete, she broke her long habit of admiring herself in secrecy.

Dressed in a light summer frock of a rich shade of apricot, rather low at the neck, with hat, gloves and shoes to match, she went out to look, for a few moments, at the wild cherry tree.

It too was in flower.

She had been standing there for five minutes or more, breathing the dry warm April air, the first tolerable breath of spring, when she heard a car coming up the hillside. Her first thought was of Boorman and the sons and she instantly turned in the act of running back to the house, in fear of being caught like a child in a guilty act.

Before she had moved five yards the car, a dark green Cortina, stopped. A voice called from it, 'Excuse me, madam' and involuntarily she stopped very sharply, halted as much by the word 'madam' as by the politeness of the voice.

She turned to see a man of about her own age, bareheaded, slightly grey at the side of the temples, looking out of the car window with something more than polite interest. The vivid discovery of her on that chunk of sordid landscape kept him completely speechless for another half minute or so and then slowly he gave an apologetic awkward sort of smile.

'Did I scare you? I'm sorry.' He laughed, awkwardly too. 'Could you direct me to the Williamson house?'

Suddenly she realised that she was actually clutching herself with both arms, almost in the act of trying to hide herself and abruptly she dropped her arms to her sides, woodenly, so that she stood there something like a clockwork doll that for some reason wouldn't work properly.

'I think it's called Beechers House or something like that.'

'Oh! no. Beechers, that's not this way. That's the next road. The one farther along.'

She lifted one hand and it might have been stiff with fright as she started to point westward along the hillside.

'Stupid of me. I thought I knew these Downs better than that.' He stared at the pig-sties, the shacks, the incredible desolation of pigs and pig-muck drying in the serene evening sun. 'But things seemed to have changed a bit up here.'

Her arm fell as if severed. It was her turn to be speechless now and there was an awkward silence of several seconds before he said:

'I used to come up here as a boy. Gathering wild strawberries.' He cast a hand at the air. 'It used to be full of flowers. Masses of them everywhere.'

He stopped, stared again at the incongruous sight of her standing there in the apricot dress against the slum background of pigs and the tall white-flowered branches of the wild cherry tree, all the time as if he couldn't believe his eyes, and then said:

'Do you live up here yourself?'

'Yes.'

He looked with calm sideways distaste at the house, half of its tiled roof replaced by rusting corrugated iron, with an attendant stack of sacks of pig-meal and a pile of old oil drums piled against one end of it as if propping it up.

'But not in that, I need hardly ask.'

Instinctively and frantically she began lying. In oppressed confusion her mind, not her body, started trembling.

'Oh! no,' she said. 'Oh! no.'

'Greatly relieved to hear it. Somehow couldn't imagine you as part of the pig world.'

To her astonishment she found herself laughing, nervously, the laugh an echo of her trembling brain.

'Oh! no. I live farther up. Over the top. You can't see it from here.'

Her nervousness was now so visibly strained that she actually began to pull off her gloves. As first one and then the other came off he couldn't fail to notice her long, well-kept hands.

'Well, I think I'll get along now,' she said. 'I was just walking back.'

Among other things he had been staring at the cherry tree. Its spring delicacy was still another part of the monstrous incongruity of the entire scene and now he suddenly saw how beautiful it was. It reminded him so much of the old days, when it was all as beautiful as that, all untouched.

'Do you mind if I walk part of the way up with you?'

In something near to panic she started biting the finger tip of her gloves. In fear of saying anything that would compromise herself her mind separated itself from her lips, so that what she actually said was not part of herself.

'Well, I'm expecting my husband. I was waiting. He may be here any moment.'

He suddenly found himself interpreting her continued open nervousness as a sort of innocence, perhaps a fear that he might behave improperly. He laughed, pleasantly this time, and said:

'Oh! I assure you I'm perfectly respectably married too.'

'Oh! I didn't mean anything like that.'

He now got out of the car, stared up the hillside and said:

'That cherry tree's marvellous.'

'Yes, it's nice.'

'It's a complete spring in itself.'

'Yes.'

'Bird cherry they call it too, sometimes, don't they?'

'I don't know. Do they?'

He smiled, this time in open appraisal of the sleek trim figure in the apricot dress, at its matching gloves and shoes and above all at the compelling combination of dark brown hair and deep clear blue eyes. It was all in such marvellous taste, he thought.

'Would you walk a little way up the road with me?'

She felt suddenly as if she were standing on the edge of a high cliff, with nothing but a vast space below her, her entire body clenched in a stark white grip of vertigo.

'Will you?' he said. 'Just a hundred yards or so. I promise I'll keep my hands in my pockets.'

In a sudden spasm of relief she smiled. He at once misinterpreted it as a gesture of invitation. Its absolute innocence had in it a disturbing intimacy.

'Actually I mustn't be long myself. I'm due at the Williamsons' for dinner.'

By now they were walking towards, under and past the cherry tree.

'Do you know them at all? The Williamsons? I'm sure you must.'

No, she said, she didn't know the Williamsons.

'I haven't seen them myself for four or five years. I've been working abroad. Persian Gulf. You can't think what it means to get back here. The English spring, I mean. That cherry tree. After the heat and the dust and – Oh! I tell you, it's marvellous.'

Every now and then, when he asked her a question, she delayed her responses. For a few seconds, not only with her lips but also her eyes, she seemed to close herself up. Withdrawn, almost fearful, she seemed to become altogether another person.

Inevitably, in this way, he began to get the impression that she was not the person she seemed to be. At once baffled and fascinated, he found himself asking questions that might shape her identity into sharper outline. Did she play bridge? The Williamsons, as he remembered it, were bridge-mad. Did she travel at all? Go to London often? He supposed she rode a bit too?

To all these questions she gave the same sort of withdrawn, delayed responses: no, she didn't play bridge, didn't ever go to London, didn't travel, didn't ride.

'Your husband farm?'

Yes, she said, her husband farmed.

'You used to be able to see the sea from here,' he suddenly said. He stopped, turned and looked back down the hill, across the pig-sties, pig-yards and the splintered strip of copse to where, far off, south-westwards, a fine thin lip of sea horizon blurred the sky. 'Ah! yes, there it is. My God, what a stunning view.'

He stood enraptured. For longer than he realised he stood in entrancement at the great pastoral expanse below him, the distant sea line, the white spire of cherry bloom. In taking it all in he tried at the same time to shut out the vile carcasses of pigs and all that pigs had done to plunder the once pure country. The impossibility of doing this suddenly made him so angry that he actually burst into a swift tirade against the blasted vandals, the scum, the oafs, who had done it all. It was utterly monstrous, foul, a sort of public sin. Didn't she agree?

Turning to her for an answer he was confronted with the most delayed of all her strange, delayed responses. She wasn't there. For a few further moments he felt himself to be the victim of some sort of trick, an April-fool illusion, the idea that she was a myth, always baffling and now evaporated.

Then suddenly he caught sight of the apricot dress, thirty yards or so farther up the hill, at a point where, at last, a new-leaved unplundered stretch of copse began. She seemed actually to be walking as if in fact she were a myth, lost, unaware of him, wanting neither to hear nor know him. He called :

'Oh! there you are. Wait!' He laughed. 'You had me fooled for a minute. I thought you'd gone —'

She neither turned nor halted. He called again and then, to his intense stupefaction, she began running, not really fast but in a disconcerting sort of flutter, at the same time pulling on her gloves.

He also started to run, then slowed himself down and finally stopped. It was the act of pulling on her gloves, he at last realized, that gave finality to her painful, curious departure.

And suddenly, painfully too, he was overcome by a curious longing and knew that he had to see her again.

She invariably, at this stage of her life, slept alone. Boorman had an almost equally invariable habit of coming home somewhere between eleven and midnight, not necessarily drunk but merely beer clumsy, to flop down on an ancient horse-hair sofa, by the kitchen stove, and snore the night away. The early, quite handsome nature of the man — as a youth he had been immensely strong, able to wield an axe with a precision that would have cut a straw within a given centimetre — had grown calloused over with a sort of muddy scab, much as a pig rolls and wallows in its own filth. The man she had at one time loved no longer existed. Nor did his departed existence even matter.

The reason for it all went back some five or six years. For the first twenty years of her married life five births and three miscarriages had kept her completely enslaved. Her bondage was so remorselessly complete that she hardly ever went out anywhere. As each child was delivered she determined it should be her last, only to discover, before wrenching herself free, that she was again imprisoned. By the time she was forty she was so fearful of life slipping away from her completely that she came to a desperate decision to break the lock of pregnancy altogether. By this time too her successive litters of pigs had given her a four-figure bank balance and it was then that she decided, for the first time, to go out and buy for herself a piece of life: a new, impossible, expensive dress. And because of it she also started to sleep alone.

After her first meeting with the man in the Cortina she lay awake for a long time, in a curious restless state that was a sort of brilliant exhaustion. Everything that had happened on the hillside, above and about the cherry tree, was etched on her mind with strokes powerful, fierce and accusatory. She convinced herself that she had done something highly foolish and wrong, that she was guilty of an act of great stupidity and even greater falsity, and that she must never do it again. The person who had walked and talked in the serene and captivating calm of the April evening was not herself. It was almost as if she had been caught in some act of great personal intimacy, naked.

In this mood of self-chastisement she fell asleep at last, slept heavily and woke two hours later than usual to the strong smell of bacon being cooked. As the sharp greasy odour of bacon floated upstairs she was increasingly aware of not feeling well. A curious nausea, causing a partial stoppage in her throat, gripped her even after she had gone downstairs, made herself a strong pot of tea and taken it back to bed with her.

It was only after some long time that she realized with any kind of accuracy what was the matter. It came to her suddenly that she was terrified of going out. She dreaded the simple exposure of daylight. The more she thought of this the stronger the grip of nausea became across her upper throat.

It was nearly midday before she forced herself to dress. When she did so she realized that April, in its treachery, had turned overnight from a fragile evening idyll into day flecked with dark rain that now and then had in it a steely bite of sleet.

For this reason she not only put on the flabby trilby, the scarf, the sackcloth apron and the gum-boots but a big old overcoat of Boorman's, something like a dark blue seaman's jacket with an enormous collar that, when upturned, buttoned close across the front, so that only her eyes, when at last she went out into the yard, were exposed to the rain.

'Feelin' bad?' Boorman said.

It was the weather, she said. She fancied she'd got a chill.

'Take aspirin,' Boorman said.

After this brief, intimate communication she groped her way across the yard. A sharp cold wind blew intermittently up the hill. Hail now and then spurted steel for a few dark minutes and then the sun stabbed with brilliance across the pig-mucked yard.

For some time she wandered aimlessly about, between sun and showers, before at last remembering that in one of the sties she had a new weakling pig, a dillin, an odd-one-out, that needed milk and care. She then went back into the house, boiled a saucepan of milk, filled a teated bottle with it and went back to the sties and the task of suckling the pig.

A stronger, brighter interval of sunshine drew her out into the yard, where she stood with the small pig cradled in her arms, half under the big greatcoat, as if she were actually suckling a baby at her breast.

In this huddled maternal attitude she again looked like a figure from some remote and ancient saga. She also felt soothed, the pain in her throat lessened. Then, as suddenly as the sun had blazed out, rain whipped down again, followed by a white battery of hail. Almost at the same moment she heard a car coming up the hill.

Standing at the door of one of the sties, still suckling the pig, she suddenly saw the car stopped in front of her, twenty yards away, on the road: the same dark green Cortina as on the evening before.

'Excuse me,' the voice from the window said again. 'Excuse me –'

A fresh white spray of hail drove the sound of the voice away and she had no word of answer. Instead she turned sharply and went behind the sty to where George, the third of her sons, was mending a pig trough.

'George, there's a man out there – wants something – see what he wants – commercial traveller I shouldn't wonder –'

George, hammer and nails in hand, wandered off. While he had gone she remained behind the sty, still clutching the piglet and its bottle, in a state very near to fright. Taut, with teeth actually clenched, the nausea in her throat gripping her more rigidly than ever, she listened for the sound of voices between squalls of hail and then at last, after a long agonizing frozen interval, heard the car turn and drive away.

When George came back he said :

'Burbling on about some woman he'd seen up here. Couldn't make head n' tail of him. Folks should mind their own bloody business – nosing round –'

After that, for some days, she went about feeling not ill but suspended between a state of brittle nausea and actual sickness. Even the nightly secret act of dressing herself up now failed for once to give the old customary pleasure. The sensuous feeling of soft garments against her body no longer excited her.

About a week later the weather, in its miraculous April fashion, abruptly improved again. An evening of serene pure light and warmth set every blackbird singing across the hillside and illuminated the black branches of the wild cherry tree as if with crystal.

In a supreme effort to shake herself out of the constriction of her inexplicable nausea she put on a plain light tweed costume, of a pale grey-blue shade, with a woollen jumper to match, and flat grey shoes. She wore no hat but tied a scarf patterned with dark blue and white roses over her head. The scarf seemed to draw out the blue of her eyes, while at the same time deepening their withdrawn intensity.

She started to walk up the hillside. She had no definite object in view. She merely walked in a state of suspended anticipation about something, her mind blank. But now and then she stopped and turned, listening for the sound of a car coming up the hill behind her.

She had been walking for a quarter of a mile or so, between deep untouched thickets of hazels and steep roadside banks yellow with primroses, when the sight of the driver of the Cortina sitting on the top of a five-barred gate brought her to a shocked halt.

Before even he could speak all her pained fright came back. Once again she felt herself to be poised on the edge of some dreadful cliff face, in the grip of a white and violent vertigo.

A moment later he jumped down from the gate, smiling, and came towards her.

'Oh! It is you. For a minute I wasn't sure. I suppose I was looking for that apricot dress.'

In speechless surprise she could do nothing but stare and this seemed to make him slightly embarrassed too. It was a marvellous evening, he said and then repeated it and then said something about how wonderful the primroses were and how the air was full of the scent of them.

'Yes,' she said. 'Yes.'

'The other night the Williamsons had bowls of them on the dinner table, pink ones and blue ones as well as the yellow. And bowls of blue and white violets too. They were wonderful under candlelight.'

'Really?'

'I'm not sure about blue primroses. Do you care for them? Somehow they're not quite right.'

Hesitantly she said she thought she preferred the wild ones.

'Me too. But I like the white violets. I suppose it sounds awfully sentimental and so on but you tend to make an awful lot of little things like that when you're abroad.'

She had never in her entire life been spoken to by anyone in this fashion and it brought to her face and her whole attitude something touchingly childlike. The silence between them crystallized into fresh embarrassment and even he for several moments could apparently think of nothing to say.

Finally he said :

'Were you going anywhere in particular? I mean –'

No, she said, no. She wasn't going anywhere in particular.

'I thought of going as far as the top. The Williamsons say there's an enormous wood of bluebells up there. Fantastic –'

They started to walk up the hill. Every now and then he half turned and looked furtively at her face and once he had a sudden explosive confession to make:

'I hope you won't think me rude but I was actually a bit disappointed when I first saw you – I mean this evening.'

'You were?'

'I mean I was looking for that apricot dress. It was so much you. So absolutely right.'

She was so touched by this that she was simply unable to trust herself to speak. Almost on the verge of tears she heard him say:

'Anyway you're here. That's the great thing.'

She found herself wanting to question him about all this, to wonder why he should speak to her on terms of such unheard-of intimacy, even to say something about his wife, but the words were impossible to frame and his next remark made her more than ever mute:

'I must say I've thought an awful lot about you.'

He suddenly stopped, turned and looked her full in the face.

'Do you mind my saying that?'

'I suppose I don't. No.'

She failed to hold his gaze and he said:

'Do you mind if I ask you your name?'

She said did it matter?

'Well, your Christian name. I can't just go on calling you the Girl in the Apricot Dress.'

'Girl?' She actually managed a light involuntary laugh at this and he was manifestly delighted and laughed too.

'All right. Lady – Lady in the Apricot Dress –'

That was even sillier, she said.

'Well then, what's your name?'

'Margaret.'

'Names don't always suit people. But that's right – that's you.'

By this time her tension had broken down a little. Suddenly it tightened again as he stopped to pick a dozen primroses from the steep roadside bank and then said, holding them out in a little bunch :

'May I? Small present for you. My name's Jack. Jack Gilbert.' He made a slight joke of it. 'The Man in Oil.'

She took the primroses and held them to her face. The touch of the extraordinarily soft petals, together with their exquisitely light perfume, had much the same effect on her as the touch of silken dresses, of lace and fur and sheer light stockings against her flesh. Instantly a start of sharp, recaptured excitement ran through her and she said, hardly able to believe her own voice :

'And what will your wife think? Talking to a strange woman? Giving her flowers –'

'We're not actually living together. I'm afraid I fibbed a bit the other evening. She came abroad with me for a time but then couldn't stand it –'

'So you think I'll fill in the gap.'

'Please don't say that.'

Suddenly she was stunned by her own effrontery and withdrew into herself, so that for the next few minutes she again spoke with nothing but those delayed responses which always so fascinated and baffled him.

'I suppose this is the beginning of the bluebell wood.' They had come by now to a chestnut wicket-gate set in a long new chestnut fence. A notice said 'Trespassers will be Prosecuted' and he said . 'They're not quite out yet. I suppose it's a trifle early.'

He leaned against the wicket-gate, facing her. Behind him the many dark young buds of a million bluebells receded into shadow under great arches of chestnut, oak and hazel. A faint, already too exquisite foretaste of their full blossoming lay with taunting lightness on the air, the tenderest breath of approaching summer.

He reached out and put his hands lightly on her shoulders. She reacted as she did when she drew on soft fresh underclothes or felt the touch of animal fur against her throat. It caused her also to breathe more deeply and quickly and suddenly her throat, completely free at last of its nausea and restriction, was full of perfume.

When he kissed her she responded thoughtlessly, mind a serene vacuum, offering neither mental nor physical resistance. His hands, first on her shoulders, then with great lightness against her thoat and then with unexplorative tenderness inside the jacket of her costume, holding her breasts, seemed to be as much part of a world of sensuous fantasy as all her evenings of secret indulgence alone with her clothes in her bedroom.

'You kiss very beautifully.'

'You shouldn't say things like that to me.'

'All right. What should I say?'

'You're also doing something else you shouldn't do.'

'Am I? Shall I take my hands away then?'

'Oh! God,' she said. 'Please –'

Suddenly a great need to be very close to him made her fold herself deeply into his arms. Obliviously, for some minutes, she made a complete surrender of herself, actually at one moment helping him lift the fringe of her jumper and draw down the straps of her slip, so that he could touch one naked breast.

'Would you make love?'

'Don't torment me like that. Please.'

'Give me one good reason why not.'

'Don't talk about reason. You meet me twice. You don't even know me. I'm practically a stranger to you and you talk like this –'

'All right, whatever you wish.' He suddenly withdrew his hands from her breasts, at the same time kissing her dispassion- ately, and slightly mockingly, on the centre of the forehead. 'I withdraw –'

'Oh! no, don't go away from me now.'

Some time later a great convulsive shudder went through her and she became blissfully, amazingly quiet. After that he con- tinued to hold her with a withdrawn response of his own until she finally gave a profound breath of relief, her head half-asleep on his shoulder.

'Would you see me again tomorrow night?'

She merely nodded and gave a low murmur.

'And would you make love?'

'I already asked you – don't torment me like that.'

'Tomorrow then.'

All this time she had been clutching, utterly unaware of it, the few frail stalks of primroses. Now she suddenly became aware of them and stared at the bruised, crushed petals, giving a short bright laugh.

'Look what I've done to my flowers.'

'We'll gather more going down the hill.'

'I don't go that way. That's not my way home.'

'No?'

'No. I go up the hill. There round the wood. That way. You don't see the house from here.'

He laughed shortly too and said she surely must be grateful for that wood. It surely sweetened the air between herself and the pig-sties. At least she was cut off from her neighbours.

'I hardly know them,' she said.

After that, every evening, they met in the wood; and now at last, every evening, she had something real, beyond fantasy, to dress for.

She tried too to wear something different every night. In this way she presented herself to him on successive waves of surprise. She seemed a different woman every time he met her. This constantly changing image of her identity inevitably gave her some air of mystery. As with her repetitive, delayed responses there was always some part of her, he felt, held back.

It was inevitable too that he should ask about her husband. What kind of a man was it, he asked, who could treat a woman like her as if – as if – half in anger, half in astonished disgust, he found himself at a loss for words.

'It all died long ago.'

When he sought to probe more deeply behind that withered

sentence she told him, at first with hesitancy and then with even more belated responses, of the evening, long ago, when she had wanted to go to a party, a wedding anniversary or something of that sort, and she had bought for it, out of almost the first of the money she made for herself, a new dress. It was a dress of vivid emerald, in taffeta, flared at the skirt, and loose, round and low at the neck. It was in fact the first of her many purchases that were brilliant to look at, sensuous to touch, exciting to wear.

'He practically tore it from my back. Said the green was unlucky, swore it made me look like a cheap, tarty bitch. I went straight upstairs and we never went to the party.'

That too, though she never told him so, was the first of her many withdrawals into the secret make-believe of dressing up. For years after that, though she didn't tell him that either, she sought solely to build for herself a life of sensuous elegance, impossibly useless beauty, that she could enjoy alone.

'The man must be a blind raving idiot. You dress with such taste. Somehow you always get everything absolutely right.'

'He isn't worth talking about.'

'Blind, puerile, raving idiot –'

'I don't come and meet you to talk about him. I don't need to talk about anything, in fact – I just come –'

Slowly, from behind yet another of her long-delayed responses, she at last confessed that what she really came for, above all, was tenderness. She had never known such tenderness. It enveloped her as sensuously and softly as the silk of her dresses. Emotionally and physically it clothed her like a second skin.

The spring, protracted, neither too warm nor too cold, seemed to hold itself back from emergence into full summer, so that the sea of bluebells in the darkening wood was still brilliant at the end of May. Nor had the primroses and drifts of white anemones and white sprays of cherry bloom fully faded either when he held her face between his two hands one evening and said:

'Got something to tell you. Miserable bit of news, I'm afraid.'

She prepared herself to make light of it. 'You don't love me any more.'

'For ever and ever. Absolutely for ever and ever. From here to eternity. For a thousand springs.'

'You're teasing me.'

'Never. No. It's this.' He purposely let his voice fall to a flat whisper. 'They may be sending me back to the Gulf.'

'May?'

'It isn't certain yet. The only thing that is certain is that I'll have to go back to town for a few days until they decide.'

'And if they do decide? Will it be for long?'

'Don't talk about it. There's nothing I can do anyway.'

Yes indeed there was, she said.

'And what is it?'

'You could love me.'

In the deep corner of the wood, lying between two big rugs he had brought from the car, she was overcome by an increasingly haunting impression that they were together, and that she was being loved, for the last time. An exhausting wave of passion in turn overwhelmed the impression briefly and she was then left in the oppressive grip of something infinitely worse: an ache of the most barren loneliness.

Much later she was to know it as something as permanently part of her as her own heart beat but that first evening the experience left her with a feeling of being completely arid, a dead sapless branch rotted to dry touchwood at the core.

She tried to make light of that too.

'In a couple of weeks you'll forget me. Off with the old and on with the new. Out of sight, out of mind.'

'Now you're being cruel to me.'

'No, no. I didn't mean that.'

'It hurts just as much to go as it does for you to be left.'

She turned with a restless impulse and pressed her naked body against him under the rug and kissed him, more in utter gratitude than anything like love or passion.

'I'm glad you said that. If you never say another word to me I'll always remember that.'

It was almost dark in the wood. A great scent of bluebells, elusive but rich, filled the twilight air. As she breathed it in she gave a long, aching, involuntary sigh.

'I'll be back in two days anyway,' he said. 'What's today? Tuesday. I'll be back Thursday. Same time, same place.'

'Same time, same place.'

Holding her breasts in his two hands he suddenly asked a final favour.

'What is it?' she said.

He drew a deep breath of his own.

'Wear that apricot dress.'

She promised she would. He began to walk down the hill to where he had parked his car. She stood watching him for a moment or two and then with one of those sudden delayed responses of hers she ran after him and impetuously threw her arms round his neck.

Impetuously too she found herself on the verge of blurting out a confession. A second or two later that too was delayed. She suppressed every word of it except the first fractured syllable and then simply stood there dumbly, caught in the trap of her own making, of her two identities, the self she was and the self she wasn't.

'What was it?' he said. 'You were going to say something.'

No, she said, she wasn't going to say anything. Not now. It was silly anyway. It wasn't important.

'You ran after me as if you were scared stiff.'

Perhaps she was, she told herself. But the impossibility of attempting to tell him that she was really two persons was again too much for her and again she stood there without a word.

He said at last that he ought to go and she said, feeling not only desperate but impossibly stupid.

'Supposing you can't get down for a day or two? Would there be some way of letting me know?'

'I could telephone.'

'We haven't got a telephone.'

'But I will come. Cross my heart and all that, if it's the last thing I do.'

'I know you will. It's just that I can't bear the thought of something that might –'

She let him go at last. It was already late. In the spring darkness she watched the headlights of the car flash full on, swing away and illuminate for a few seconds the white branches of the cherry tree, the pig-stics, the pig-yards and the shabby corrugated roof of the house before disappearing altogether.

Then she walked down the road. She walked stiffly and slowly, head up, eyes staring directly ahead, like a child walking on a tight-rope, frozen with the terror of falling.

Nearly a month went by. The last of the bluebells faded completely in the wood. The blossom from the cherry tree thinned and faded too from the black branches.

Soon the many greens of the May landscape merged gradually into one single green, a great leaf blanket, so that even as early as eight o'clock it was almost dark in the wood as she stood there, always in the apricot dress, and waited for the sound of a car coming up the hill.

During this time she again went about feeling not really ill but suspended between a brittle nausea and actual sickness. By day she slopped about the pig-yards, carrying swill, shovelling dung, suckling some weakling of a piglet too feeble to fend for itself, her identity lost under the sack apron, the mud-caked boots, the floppy ancient hat.

On a day towards the end of June she was backing out the old Ford truck, preparing to load into it half a dozen pigs, when she saw the green Cortina driving up the hill. As the car went past the gate of the farm-yard she caught her first glimpse of Jack Gilbert for nearly a month. He was wearing a light-weight biscuit-coloured suit and a yellow and green club tie. The neat freshness of his appearance at once caused her to break out in a cold sweat, so that she stood again as if on the edge of a cliff, in the grip of a cold white vertigo.

The car stopped two hundred yards up the hill. She stood in the road and watched Gilbert get out, light a cigarette and then stand smoking it, quickly, in nervous, impatient snatches. Then suddenly he threw the half-smoked cigarette down, crushed it with the heel of his pale brown suède shoe and began to walk up the hill.

Even as he started walking he lit another cigarette and began to smoke that too in quick nervous gasps. Some twenty yards further on he abruptly stopped, turned, seemed about to change his mind over something and then as abruptly went on. If at that moment she was within his line of vision he failed utterly to notice it. She might have been a tree stump, a gate post, even another pig standing there on the roadside.

A wild impulse to rush into the house, change into a dress of some sort and run up the hillside after him flared and died in her in a matter of seconds, leaving her ashen. She endured for some few minutes longer the torment of the old dilemma she had created for herself, the fraudulent trap of being two people, and then she started to drag herself slowly up the hill.

Rather less than ten minutes later she met him coming back down the road. He was still smoking in short violent snatches. As they passed each other he took the cigarette from his mouth, muttered a half-audible good morning and then threw the cigarette away.

In that moment a second and even wilder impulse brought her to the very edge of snatching off her scarf and hat. It failed completely simply because every atom of strength ebbed from her arms and hands. She found herself in a state of sudden bloodless paralysis, unable to take even another step up the road.

Without even a second glance at her he went on down the hill. It seemed like an hour rather than only a minute or so before she gathered strength enough to turn and look after him. When she finally did so he had reached the car.

Before getting into it he stood for some moments beside it and lit yet another cigarette. As his lighter flared it had the effect on her of an electric switch being sharply pressed and in that moment she snatched off her scarf and hat, ruffled both hands through her dark brown hair and then stood there completely motionless, bare headed.

With almost a final glance of indifference in her direction he killed the flame in his lighter, thrust it into his pocket and put his hand on the handle of the car door. A moment later he seemed to be struck by an infinitely brief flash of interest in her. For a few seconds it seemed remotely possible that he might have recognized her. Then he suddenly threw the last of his many cigarettes on the road, crushed it underfoot, got into the car and drove away. In that same moment she lifted her hand, half as if to wave, and then let it fall dead at her side.

It was the last of her delayed responses. Not even seeing it, he drove on, down the hill, towards the motorway and the metallic beetles, and at last out of sight.

Some Other Spring

IT was going to be rather something, he told himself, for the tenth time or so, to see the children again after nearly two years. They might well have changed out of all recognition; they might well be strangers.

It was partly for that reason he had left his car in the village and decided to walk the rest of the way, a quarter of a mile or so, across the fields. He would go in – no, sort of saunter in, quite casually, as if in fact the house were still his own – through the garden, by the back way. It seemed altogether too formal to use the front door. You couldn't very well knock and say 'Hullo, good afternoon, excuse me, I've come to pay my visit to the children. I'm allowed to see them once a month, if you remember. You know, the court order. Yes, I know I haven't – yes, it's been some time – I hope you got my letter. I did write to confirm.'

The old Saunders place next door looked well, he thought, across the fields. The black and white front stood out in the August sun like a piece of iced cake against the black background of pines. He always envied the Saunders place, so marvellously well kept, so permanent, so immemorial somehow, so secure: all due, of course, to Elspeth, who looked after her father as efficiently as she looked after the garden, the house, the accounts, the cooking and everything else. She would have made someone an awfully good wife, Elspeth, he always thought: nice looks, charming, pleasant, affectionate, good taste, good clothes, good manners, good cook, good everything. He simply couldn't think why she had never made it. He supposed she might well have given up the thought of it now. But then, in a way, perhaps it was no loss: you had to have women like Elspeth, who ran their fathers' houses with efficiency, remembered birthdays, became miraculous godmothers and were always faultless friends. After all they couldn't all be wives.

The surrounding countryside looked pretty immemorial too, he thought. It was so long since he had seen it that he had forgotten how perfectly the low fold of meadows gave way to strips of cornland, the barley almost as white as the chalk on which it grew, and the glowing beauty of the dark beechwoods above and beyond.

If these old familiar things seemed to surprise him pleasantly the sight of his own house – it wasn't his own any more, but for some reason he couldn't get out of the habit of thinking it was – grated on him, it always had, with irritation. You could see even from a distance that it fairly sprouted shabbiness. Even the curtains of the window in the east gable hadn't been pulled back : that old, old bone of contention. Why on earth couldn't Carrie remember?

Naturally, of course, because she was Carrie. She was made like that. He could look at it dispassionately now. Untidiness, shabbiness, slopping about, come-easy, go-easy, dust and cobwebs : she loved it all; to her it was all, in a sense, romantic. A house in the country was merely a glorious ramshackle plaything for messing about with, whereas he himself had just as naturally wanted it to be ordered, civilized, a pattern.

For instance, the garden. He had been most passionately keen on the garden. He had gone to great expense in making, among other things, a rock-garden, with specially imported stone, and a lily pond. In no time the lily pond was full of rusty toys, old bricks, ice-cream cartons, ghastly little tricycles. The children dug sand castles among the rocks. They played absolute hell with his beautifully nurtured gentians.

Carrie thought this natural, even funny. They must be allowed, she fiercely maintained, to be themselves, to give expression to this and that, to run free.

'But God, the wretched pool looks like a bomb-site. Look at the mess – look at the tin-cans –'

'Then let it look like a bomb-site. To them –'

'But damn it, hell, it isn't a bomb-site. It's a pool. A lily pool. I paid good hard-earned money to have the thing made and now look what the little horrors –'

'And how are they to know that? They don't know. They can't differentiate between a lily pool and a bomb-site. To them it's merely a place. They can't differentiate –'

'Oh! don't keep using words like differentiate.'

'Oh! and why not?'

'Oh! it's sort of councilese – sort of – well, why don't you just say "tell the difference"? – I don't know, it's sort of suburban –'

'Sort of, sort of, sort of – My God, it's no more suburban than that!'

By now he had reached the back boundary of the garden. He paused by the privet hedge. He seemed to see them still, the little perishers. He saw Nigel, the boy, actually riding a filthy tricycle through the lily pond, crushing lilies as they floated in full bloom, with Gilian, the girl, towed on behind in what seemed to be some sort of wretched fish-box on wheels. They were laughing uproariously, almost idiotically, and Carrie was laughing with them. No wonder he had hated and loved them; no wonder the end had come.

'You've got a sort of bead-frame mind, you have. Everything's got to be neat and in rows. Proper colours and added up. All nice and tidy and mathematical.'

He was almost, at that moment, on the verge of turning back. It seemed the height of stupidity, suddenly, to rake it all up again. Could children change? He doubted it. Once there, the character could only manifest itself accordingly; like a plant, it was fixed : poisonous or not, fragrant or otherwise.

All of a sudden he was bothered by something about the hedge. It was somehow different. That end of the garden had always been a rampant wilderness, deep in nettles, a maze of bryony and elderberry everywhere. It was where the tin cans came from.

Now he was aware not merely of an air of change, but even

of order. To his infinite astonishment the hedge had been smoothly clipped. The elderberry bushes that he remembered as being like untidy purple autumnal umbrellas had been laid low. The wicket gate, half way along it, had actually been painted, the slats alternatively green and white.

With his hand on the latch of the gate he was halted by an oppressive thought. Had Carrie married again and not told him? Or had she now a boy-friend, for whom the new-painted garden gate was as essential a part of her attraction as the lipstick on her face? He suddenly felt, in any case, a dreadful stranger, an intruder, cold and out of it.

He supposed, now, that that was why she had invited him to tea : family gathering and so on. It would ease the situation : everyone on best behaviour. This, at least, was a relief. In such a situation he wouldn't have to play games, make pet mice out of handkerchiefs or pretend, as he jogged the children on his knee, that he was a raspberry jam factory.

He pushed open the gate and went into the garden that surprised him, like the hedge, with its air of orderliness. Gone were not only the elderberry bushes, but the tin cans. Shrubs, with an underplanting of silver foliage in many shapes, had supplanted them. The old brick wall that ran behind and beyond had been cleaned up and planted with a yellow *Mermaid* rose, still in full bloom, and a clematis that erupted over the crest of it in thick purple pennants, warm velvet in the August sun.

'And Good God, an *Abutilon megopotanicum*. Incredible. What on earth's that doing here?' He stood staring at a shrub hung with many red and black and yellow bells, in shape not unlike a fuchsia, and felt a sharp strange pang of envy. Some new influence had been at work all right. How otherwise had she ever managed to plant that? It wasn't even hardy.

He started to finger the shrub's slender leaves, jealous now not only of the shrub but of Carrie. In a way it wasn't quite fair. He had always wanted to grow that particular *abutilon* but had never really dared to risk it. The three-coloured bells were so beautiful. They were like little pagodas. He fingered the leaves again. One might, he supposed, have a shot with cuttings?

'Are you trying to pinch bits from the garden?'

'Oh! no, I really wasn't doing that. Oh! no, I was just admiring.'

He turned and saw his daughter, Gilian, standing on the edge of the path. He supposed she was seven now, or thereabouts. He couldn't accurately remember. She seemed awfully tall, anyway, he thought, and was wearing tartan trews, a red shirt-blouse and her blonde hair in a horse-tail.

'No, you really mustn't think I was stealing. Just admiring, that's all.'

'That's what all the people said at the garden party. Oh! no, nobody was putting bits in their handkerchiefs. Just admiring, that's all. Did you want Mummy?'

'I'm your father.'

For a moment he fully expected her to say something like 'I might have known', but then, as the cold notion of being a stranger suddenly enveloped him again, he heard the familiar voice of Carrie, rather high-pitched as usual, saying as she came across the lawn:

'Ah! there you are. No wonder we couldn't see you – creeping in by the back way, eh?'

He refrained from commenting, although strongly and briefly tempted, on the word creeping, and merely said:

'Afraid I was caught in the act. Hullo.'

'Well, after all, there is a front door bell.'

He stood facing Carrie, not knowing what to say. He hadn't seen her, either, for nearly two years. She was very brown and rather leaner in the face, he thought. Her very light blonde hair was done in that chewed-off fashion that seemed to be so popular at the moment. He didn't like it. His daughter stood apart.

He felt he ought to refer, somehow, to the incident of the abutilon. He said he supposed that Gilian hadn't recognized him.

'Oh! nonsense. Of course she knew you. She's been hopping about expecting you all day.'

'Yes? I must say the abutilon took me by surprise.'

'The what?'

'The abutilon. The thing growing up the wall. I must say you've done wonders with the wall.'

'Oh! that. That's not me, I'm afraid. That's Charles. He's responsible for all that.'

Well, damn it, he thought. He felt she might have told him. He supposed, really, that he hadn't any real right to know of – well, any new set-up, liaison or whatever it was – but he was after all the father of the children.

Who was this Charles? Another gardener, it seemed. That struck him as pretty rich. He and Carrie had practically arrived at dagger point because of what she called his bead-frame mind, his meticulous passion for the straight line, proper colours and everything added up, and now there was this Charles and the garden as neat and ordered as a park.

He noticed that the children weren't dashing about it everywhere on those damned tricycles either. He looked hastily at Gilian, who in return gave him, shyly, a side-long glance and a smile. She too, like the garden, was incredibly tidy, so utterly different from the sloppy, muddy little horror who had trailed about his lily pool that again he felt a stranger, cold, out of it all.

Then he remembered that, of course, he was a stranger. He didn't belong here. He heard Carrie ask if he wouldn't like to see the rest of the garden before tea and as they began to walk across the lawn, itself as smooth and even as a sheet of green baize, his eye caught in the middle distance a great orange crowd of tiger lilies, curled turbanned heads flaming against some artemesia-like cloud of grey.

He was at once stricken by a pang of jealousy. At the same time he had to admire the rightness of the combination, of the contrast between gold flower and grey leaf, fire and smoke. It was all most effective, if anything too damned effective.

'Oh! that's Charles again. Anything you see out of the ordinary, that's Charles.'

46

He now supposed that Charles would, of course, be at tea. Conversation would have to be made with Charles: he would have to be polite. In irritation he wished he had never come. It was all a bit deceitful, not quite fair, not playing the game.

'I think you're awfully like your photograph.'

He discovered that Gilian was walking very close to him. Her airy light horse-tail was almost transparent in the sun. He was aware of a presence very feminine and slightly strange too, not at all daughterly. Her sharp blue eyes, though shy, never left him.

'Oh! I take awful photographs. Which photograph was that?'

'The one where you're gathering wild strawberries. Up on the hills.'

'Oh! yes.'

'You've got your handkerchief knotted over your head because it was so hot. Don't you remember?'

Children had awful memories, he thought. They remembered the most ridiculous, impossible details.

'Oh! you remember that,' Carrie said. 'Even I remember that day.'

'We gathered five pounds and afterwards we made jam and it didn't set very well.' Gilian kept him in a sharp, prolonged side-long glance, now partly in recollection, part in scrutiny. 'You can't go up there now. They've ploughed it all up.'

'Oh! yes I remember now.' He didn't remember at all – or just, perhaps, very vaguely.

Glad to change the subject, he noted a new blaze of fire across the garden: a burning vermilion cluster of horns with small white honeycombs of dahlias below. Again the contrast was very striking, very right. He supposed it was a salvia of some sort?

'Oh! you must ask Charles. He knows all about names. I'm hopeless. You know, I think you and old Charles might have a great deal in common.'

Old Charles, he noted with irritation and then saw that she was smiling at him. He noticed the particular quality of the

47

smile with surprise. Formerly it too might have been an irritant. It was an old habit of hers to smile when acid, even bitter. Now there was no trace of acrimony.

'You must come and see my garden. I've got a piece all to myself.'

'Oh! yes, you must see Gilian's garden. She's mad about her garden.'

'When, now?'

'Oh! when she's ready. You're very honoured. Even I don't get asked.'

'After tea, will you come?'

'Yes, of course.'

Speaking of tea, Carrie said, she thought they might go into the house now. Where was Nigel? Would Gilian run and find him? He found himself recoiling coldly at the name Nigel. He had always hated that name. It had been a great source of conflict, that name, a great breeder of rows, but in the end he had given in.

'Oh! he'll come, won't he?' Gilian stood very close to him again, still holding him with that sharp, shy, sidelong glance. 'He never comes if you go and fetch him.'

'Oh! Here's Elspeth anyway. Oh! there you are, Elspeth — nice and early, good.'

Charles, he noted now to himself, didn't have all the monopoly of taste and the rightness of doing things. As Elspeth came across the lawn in a light cream linen suit piped at the edges with what seemed to be thinnest stalks of bright green reed she also seemed to have the quality of some well-placed flower. Her deep natural brown hair was burning and sombre in the sun.

'We all know about your dreadful memory, but don't go and say you don't remember Elspeth.'

'Of course I remember Elspeth. Vividly. Is that the right thing to say, Elspeth?'

'Of course. Only there was a time when you used to kiss me too.'

48

Elspeth held up her face to be kissed. He duly kissed it, on both cheeks, with polite affection. At the same time he remembered that he had kissed neither Carrie nor his daughter. It was perhaps remiss. On the other hand there was Charles.

'Oh! that's more like it.' The eyes of Elspeth were like moist, gold-brown shells. 'How are you? Let's have a look at you.' She stood back to appraise him. Her smile, like the cheeks he had just kissed so lightly, was smooth and warm. 'Pass with honours.'

'Putting on a little weight, I thought,' Carrie said.

'Oh! Carrie, nonsense. Not a gramme.'

'Have you put on weight? You have.'

'Oh! why is everyone so obsessed with weight?' he said. 'If you must know I've lost three ounces since yesterday. I've had my hair cut.'

Elspeth laughed brightly at this, with rich amusement. Carrie seemed, however, not to think it funny and looked at him with what, in the past, he had sometimes called that old spoon look of hers. It was tarnished and unreflective.

'Well and what do you think of the garden? Don't you think we've livened it up?'

'We?'

'Oh! it's Charles and Elspeth who've done it all. You know how mad keen Elspeth always was. Charles and she talk the language. Just like you do.'

The voice of Carrie was again an irritant. They were all walking across the lawn now, Gilian still close to him, still watching. The old white French rose, *Madame Alfred Carrière*, was flowering beautifully, for the second time, on the house wall, and for some reason he again thought of the abutilon.

'Oh! yes that was from a cutting of mine,' Elspeth said.

'Everything's from Elspeth's cuttings. Elspeth brings them and Charles bungs them in.'

He had no idea, for a few moments, what to say, and walked on in silence. Then something made him remember Gilian. Her eyes were still fixed on him and he said:

'What about your garden? Does Charles help in your garden too?'

'Oh! no. My garden's my own.'

*

They would have tea, Carrie said, on the lawn, under the big cherry tree. She would put the kettle on; everything was ready on a tray.

It was close beyond the cherry tree where the lily pond had been. He looked for it now in vain. A bed of heathers, with dwarf conifers and clumps of blue-grey grass and a pocket or two of miniature scarlet roses had taken its place.

'Oh! yes I'm afraid the pool's gone for a Burton. That was an early casualty. The aquatic things grew like mad and smothered the water-lilies and then the cherry leaves came down and in the end there just wasn't any water. It was an awful mess. Charles couldn't have that. He filled it in.'

Silently he mourned the pool. It had been rather a pet of his, the pool. Perhaps it was badly sited there, too near the tree, but all the same—

'Will you be long, Carrie? Can I help? If not, I'd rather like to show Roger that thing I snaffled from the old Abbey garden. The red thing. The one nobody's been able to name.'

'As long as you don't drag it out too long. India or China?'

'China, I think. I know Roger likes China. He always did.'

The eyes of Gilian watched him like those of a dog waiting to be tempted with a morsel of food, for the snap of a leash, for a run across the fields.

'I do want you to see this thing. Nobody has a notion what it is. I suppose you could send it to Kew and they'd know. How does the garden strike you?'

'It seems larger somehow.'

'Oh! that's Charles. He's done a lot of clever cutting down, Charles. Opening up vistas and that sort of thing.'

He suddenly felt the compulsive pull of two forces: a growing impatience with Charles and a submission to the deep brown warmth of Elspeth's voice, urging him to look now at a long serpentine valley of azaleas where once, he knew, nothing had ever grown but gooseberries. Of course the azaleas were over now, but in the spring – it had been marvellous in the spring.

'Did I hear a rumour that you were going to be married again?'

He knew it was a try-on; he knew there was no such rumour. He merely said :

'No, no. And you? What about you?'

'Oh! I still keep house for Father.'

'Still? It isn't good for you.'

'I suppose not.'

She caught his arm, guiding him away from the azaleas. The new plan of the garden was all unfamiliar to him. It wasn't his any longer and he felt more than ever a stranger to it all, a cold intruder.

'Well, there it is. What do you make of it? I just snaffled a couple of cuttings and in no time Charles had it going.'

He was coming to the point where, he thought, he could cheerfully have strangled Charles. The shrub he now saw before him, four or five feet high, flowering with a curious blood-red tassel, slightly flamboyant, was very beautiful. It was totally unfamiliar too but he said :

'It's that Obedient Plant thing, isn't it? You push the flowers round and they stay where you put them.'

'Oh! I never thought of that.'

'Try pushing the flowers round. Swivel them. They ought to stay where you put them. Like the hands of a clock.'

He watched her fingers on the blood-red flowers. He saw her touch and twist and turn them, this way and that, and then saw that they were not like the hands of a clock. They didn't obey; they didn't stay where you put them.

'So it isn't that, after all.'

'No, it can't be that. To me it always looks like a sub-tropical snapdragon. But of course it's not. No other thoughts?'

No, he said, he was afraid he had no other thoughts. It was something of a mystery. Of course she could, he suggested, always go back to the garden she had pinched it from and ask there.

She laughed, throwing her head back, and the sound was as warm and tawny as the tiger lilies he had seen, not long since, burning across the garden.

'Supposing I took a flower and looked it up and dropped you a line?'

Oh! no, she said, she thought that would rather spoil it now. It would be better to let it stay as it was, something of a mystery. It might probably turn out to be some awfully ordinary thing, a rampant weed from Kenya or somewhere. One day you'd meet someone who would laugh in your face and say 'What, that thing? We could never get rid of it.'

Her alternate laughing and talking suddenly stopped. The garden, shut off at some distance from the house, became very quiet. A profound silence sang all about them. The warm brown eyes encompassed him and she said:

'Shouldn't ask this, I suppose. But why the long time coming back? Oh! it's difficult, I suppose.'

'I wasn't exactly encouraged.'

'Well, you're encouraged now.'

She put her face to his, giving him no more than the shadow of a kiss on the side of it.

'Well, now tea I suppose.'

'Well, yes, I suppose –'

She started to walk away. For a moment or two he felt left in air. Then he felt a powerful urge to take her by the shoulders and turn her back. After all he was free. There was nothing, not a thing, to hold him now.

'Well, come on. You heard what Carrie said. Don't drag it out too long.'

He joined her without a word and together they went up through the new azalea walk, crimson here and there with a burning leaf or two, and so to the lawn and across to the house.

He became aware, half way across the lawn, of a waiting figure.

'Gilian's on the watch for you.'

'So I see.'

From the house Carrie appeared, carrying a silver teapot and plate of cream-cheese sandwiches. She smiled and said Oh! there they were and how perfectly they had timed it and her voice was dry.

'Milk or lemon, Roger?'

'Oh! lemon,' Elspeth said. 'He always did.'

'I'll have lemon today too,' Gilian said.

Set half in sun, half in shade, the table with its shining cups and china gave a twisted sort of sparkle.

'Well, did you solve the great mystery?'

No, he said, he was afraid he'd made a wrong guess.

'Obedient Plant, he thought,' Elspeth said. 'But it turned out not. It didn't obey.'

Well, Carrie said, if it beat Charles it would beat anybody.

'What is an Obedient Plant?' Gilian said.

He started to explain about the Obedient Plant. A certain feeling of futility about the explanation suddenly made him impatient and he was on the point of stopping the whole thing when he saw the eyes of his daughter, large and transfixed, holding him as if mesmerized. Hastily he renewed the explantion, saying how the flowers could be turned this way and that, wherever you liked, and would stop where you left them.

'How clever. How did you find out about a thing like that?'

Oh! he supposed he'd swotted it up at some time, heard of it somehow.

'I think it's marvellous.'

'I can't imagine,' Carrie said, 'where Nigel's got to. Gilian, go and look for him again.'

'I looked. He said he wouldn't come. He's playing with water outside the dog-kennel.'

'He's been truculent, that boy, all day. Apologies for your son – he's sometimes a bit like that.'

Without a word he picked up his spoon and jabbed at the lemon in his China tea. Apologies : as if the truculence, the refusal to come to table, were all his fault. He was relieved, however, rather than offended. One of the things he had dreaded more than anything was to meet the boy. It imposed on him an obligation only equalled by the necessity, sooner or later, of meeting Charles.

'Oh! by the way,' Elspeth said, 'I brought a few seedlings of the other abutilon over. The mauve one, *vitifolium*. I put them in the greenhouse. You know it, Roger, don't you?'

'It's lovely.'

'I really prefer it to the *megapotanicum*.'

'I think I do too.'

'We had it once before but the last bad winter killed it. Now the new one has set seed.'

'We had it here too and something killed it. Some truculent axe, I think.'

At once the tea-table seemed to flame. An interval of what seemed the better part of a minute, but in reality only a few seconds, ignited and seared the air. He waited for yet a further whip of it to reach him from Carrie's tongue but she merely poured more hot water into the tea-pot and Elspeth said :

'I think they need over-wintering inside. They're that bit tender.'

'I'll tell Charles.'

The flame that had momentarily and dramatically flashed across the table by now was dead, leaving empty ashen air behind.

'I thought I heard the gate,' Carrie suddenly said. 'Go and see. It's perhaps the postman.'

'It could be Charles,' Elspeth said.

'Oh! no. He won't be here today.'

Well that, he thought, was at least considerate. Thank God for that. At least the ordeal of meeting the universal Charles needn't bother him any more.

Gilian, he noticed, hadn't gone to the gate. He helped himself to a third cream-cheese sandwich. She took one too. As she did so he noticed, surprisingly for the first time, that she was wearing two circular badges on the lapel of her blouse: one scarlet and one gold.

'What are your badges for?'

'One's for good conduct and one's for the week's progress.'

'But you're on holiday.'

'Yes, but I'm just wearing them today.'

He ought, he supposed, to talk about schools and progress and things like that. On the other hand – He went to drink more tea and found that his cup was empty.

'Let me fill you up. Was it right? Enough sugar?'

'Delicious. Just one lump.'

Yes, schools. That was important.

'Do you like school?'

'You've touched on a sore subject,' Carrie said. 'No, she doesn't.'

'Oh! no, that's not true. I do and I don't.'

'Well, we were all like that. I remember –'

He stopped. He saw that not only was Gillian looking at him, eyes minutely watchful, but that Elspeth was watching too.

'Well, go on. I thought we were going to hear something terribly important –'

'No, no. Just that I – you know how school is.'

There was a kind of light Madeira sponge cake, with jam filling, on the table. Would he care for some? No, he didn't think he would, really, he wasn't for sweet things all that much. Nor, it seemed, was Gilian.

'Strange, that,' Elspeth said. 'I notice all children are like that, nowadays. They're not much for sweet things. They all go for savouries. I've got a niece of three who gorges stuffed olives. I think I was twenty before I tried a stuffed olive and then I didn't like it.'

'Oh! I hate stuffed olives. I hate savouries and fishy things and all that. I hate –'

'Now, now,' Carrie said. 'Don't let's have a hate day.'

'Hate day?' he said.

'Oh! yes, we have hate days,' Carrie said. 'One day this week it was horses. The day after that, circuses, wasn't it? Yesterday it was Charles, of all people.'

'Well, I do hate Charles.'

'Now nobody on earth,' Elspeth said, 'could hate Charles. Charles is an absolute –'

'I hate him. He never lets me do anything. He's always mean and snappy and you don't have to touch things.'

God, he thought, this was – He sipped slowly at his tea. A leaf from the cherry-tree, prematurely crimson, floated suddenly down in the windless air and settled lightly in the centre of the tea-table, making Elspeth say :

'Oh! leaves falling already. Don't say it's going to be an early autumn.'

'I think that's the one thing that makes Charles really bad-tempered,' Carrie said. 'Leaves. Sweeping-up. He hates them. They're so endless.'

'Well, this year we've gone in for one of those patent sweeper-up gadgets. You must borrow it.'

'Ah! that means you'll monopolize him. I think you've got even more leaves than we have.'

'Well, we'll have to toss up for him again, that's all.'

In mystification he sat mute. It struck him as being more than a bit liberal, two women tossing up for the husband of one of them, and again he felt out of it all, a cold intruder in a strange world. Was that the reason, perhaps, for the hatred? It was understandable. He was near enough to hating Charles himself.

'How much do these things cost?' Carrie said. 'I might as well get one too. He hates borrowing things.'

'Oh! no don't go to that expense. After all we share him. Let's share the gadget.'

'All right, if you say so. By the way, since the days are drawing in, won't it soon be time we changed the time-table? – you have him in the mornings and me in the afternoons.'

The mystification on his face evidently turned to astonishment, then stupefaction. He felt positively sullen. The intrusion on peculiar private affairs made him wish to God, once again, that he had never come. A certain warmth he had hitherto felt for Elspeth curled up and died inside himself like a dry worm. It wasn't any wonder there was hatred.

'Roger, you look terribly thoughtful.'

Thoughtful? He started to say something about not being a particularly cynical man but of course if sharing Charles gave any satisfaction – then his sentence died too, cut dead by Elspeth and Carrie laughing.

'Roger, you're a scream – did you really think Carrie and I? –'

'In the *mornings* too! – God, I'm never any good in the mornings anyway.'

'Oh! me, of course, I'm terrific. Can you see me? – all voluptuous in slacks and a wind-cheater, waiting for Charles in a wheel-barrow.'

It was not, he thought, funny. He stared at his empty tea-cup, at the garden and then, quickly and sullenly, at Gilian. She in return hardly looked at him. There was no change in her face even when Carrie and Elspeth burst out laughing again, so loudly and high-spirited that it mocked him. He felt like the victim of some bad, practical joke.

'Roger, what an idea – you didn't really think –'

'Well, perhaps we should try it some time,' Elspeth said. She was still laughing, bright tawny eyes quite flashing in their amusement. 'I never thought of it – hullo, where's Gilian hopped off to?'

The joke of Charles died out slowly, in repeated splutters, a damp but irresponsible firework. For him, too, the afternoon died. No, he wouldn't have more tea, thank you.

'I'm sorry you saw dear old Charles in such a bad light,' Carrie said. Her voice now had that slight edge to it, fine with acidity. 'I hope our poor old gardener is now acquitted without a stain on his character.'

'It was a genuine mistake.'

The aftermath of laughter was cold. He tried to think of an excuse for going very soon, without seeming to be too impossibly stiff, and was very suddenly struck by the thought of the boy playing outside the dog-kennel.

'I suppose I ought to say hullo to Nigel before I go.'

'Oh! you're not going yet? Go and find him yourself – he'd like that. There's plenty of time.'

He got up from the table and walked across the lawn. Behind him he caught the echo of yet one more cackle of laughter, but when it died the afternoon was gripped in quietness.

The dog-kennel in the yard behind the kitchen was empty, graced by neither boy nor dog. He looked at it for a few moments, feeling empty too. He remembered the yard as a dumping ground for buckets, heaps of sand, bits of iron bedsteads lashed together in grotesque shapes of planes and cars, old bath tins labouring in sordid puddles or beached across the waste of unswept asphalt.

Now it was all carefully swept; there were even tubs of scarlet and pink geraniums set about it; the asphalt had been replaced by broad flags of paving stone.

He walked through the yard and out to the kitchen garden beyond. That too was neat and orderly : a barrack square filled with platoons of carrots and onions, beetroot and beans, enough potatoes to feed an army.

He went out of it by a wooden wicket gate at the far side. Beyond it, in a triangle of holly and briar and laurel, the garden ended, and it was almost a relief to see it end half in neglect, hidden away, in secret disorder.

In the centre of it sat Gilian.

'This is my garden. Charles won't let me have it anywhere else.'

'It's nice here. All on its own.'

'Do you like it?'

An oblong plot of earth had been scraped out and lined with

flints, half bricks and lumps of stone. He stared at it for some time, not speaking.

'I've got candytuft in there, but it hasn't come up yet. And Iceland poppies. They're really for next year.'

'Are they carrots coming up there?'

'Carrots? No, that's supposed to be larkspur.'

'It looks like carrots.'

'Oh! no, I don't think so. I hope not. I sowed Chinese pinks too. That's what it said on the packet. Chinese. Do you think it's them coming up?'

'No, I think that's grass there.'

She had only just made the garden, she said: only a week or two ago. It really hadn't got started yet. Everything seemed to be so slow coming up. Should they be so slow?

'It doesn't get an awful lot of light in here.'

'No, I know. But it will later. In the winter. When the leaves fall.'

'Oh! yes. And in the spring. Plants respond to light as much as anything. You'll see an awful difference in the spring.'

He stooped and pulled up a root of groundsel and threw it aside.

'Oh! must you pull that up? I thought it was a flower.'

'Oh! I'm sorry,' he said. 'I didn't think you wanted it.'

He would send her packets of seeds, he said, as if in compensation, and she said thank you, she would like that. She re-arranged a few stones along the edge of the plot and picked up a piece of broken glass or two and threw them away.

'You thought I was stealing bits from the garden,' he said. 'Rather funny.'

It disturbed him that she didn't say anything in answer. Perhaps it wasn't funny. He felt it time to go. Would she come too? He ought to go and say good-bye to her mother.

'No, I'll stay here. I've got quite a bit to do.'

'Well, I'll say good-bye then.'

He thought at first, foolishly, that he would shake hands with her. He actually extended his right hand and then dropped it to his side. Then she slightly lifted her face and he kissed it on both cheeks and it was almost, for a moment, as if he were saying good-bye to Elspeth instead.

'I must go now. Good-bye.'

'Good-bye. You won't forget the seeds?'

'No, I won't forget the seeds. What seeds would you like?'

'Oh! I don't know. Not really. Anything.'

'Well, you say and I'll send them.'

'No, you choose. Anything you like. You choose.'

'All right. I'll try to send some good things. Good-bye now.'

'Good-bye.'

For some reason it was the thought of Elspeth, not Gilian, that rode light and uppermost in his mind as he crossed the kitchen garden, then the yard, and came out to the lawn and flower beds beyond. He had been profoundly glad of Elspeth, without really realising it, all afternoon. Elspeth had helped enormously. Of course the misunderstanding about Charles was all perfectly ridiculous; genuine mistake though it was, all his fault. The idea of two women sharing – it was all preposterous but now he could, perhaps, seeing that it was all over, share the joke.

By the time he reached the lawn there was no one in sight. The tea-table was cleared. The lawn was empty. Then he saw the figure of Carrie, waiting on the steps of the house.

'I'm sorry. It was Gilian. I had to see the garden.'

'You're very honoured. I told you. Did you see Nigel?'

'No, he wasn't there.'

'I see.'

'Oh! and has Elspeth gone? Oh! surely not. I wanted to say good-bye.'

'She suddenly fled. She suddenly remembered she had some cream to pick up in the village. It was nearly half-past five.'

He once again felt out of it all, cold, a stranger intruding.

'What did she have to rush for?'

'Oh! she's like that sometimes.'

'I didn't say good-bye.'

'She said to tell you good-bye. And if you ever had a thought about the name of that plant –'

'Oh! yes. Did you say honoured? Why?'

'Oh! even I haven't seen the garden yet.'

He stared across the empty lawn, towards the tawny flame of tiger lilies with their attendant silver sprays, at the purple burning clematis on the wall. It was all splendidly kept, in beautiful order. There was hardly a leaf, a twig, a blade of grass out of place.

'What was the garden like?' Carrie said.

He paused before answering. He must go pretty soon. There was nothing to wait for.

'She has great plans for it,' he said. He remembered suddenly her watching eyes, her long, waiting silences. 'It should be marvellous in the –'

'In what?'

'Oh! in the spring.'

Or if not in the spring, he thought, some other time: some other spring.

The World Upside-Down

THE first time Miss Olive Stratton put on odd stockings, one a greenish brown, the other a shade of rusty red, was purely by accident, as she hurriedly dressed herself in the twilight of a winter morning. But when daylight came and she could see better it suddenly struck her how curiously attractive, even striking, the odd stockings were. They might even be a reason, she thought, for making men look at her legs more often, more closely and perhaps with more appreciation. They were not very good legs and the more she could do to improve them, she felt, the better.

Nor was her face at all an exceptional one. It resembled, as much as anything, a piece of rather coarse yellowish flannel. The grey eyes were dark, as if with bruises, underneath. For this reason she wore tinted spectacles of a smoky rose colour. Her black hair was also coarse and would in fact have been slightly grey if she hadn't regularly tinted that too.

After the discovery of the stockings she began to go to work every morning wearing one stocking of one colour and one of another. Sometimes she chose blue and green; sometimes red and yellow; once purple and brown. On one occasion she even went so far as to wear a green stocking and a red shoe on one leg and a red stocking and a green shoe on the other. On another occasion, a morning of black snowy slush, she wore odd calf-length boots, one white and one black, with a pair of gloves matching them but as it were in opposition.

In spite of all this the desired effect of making men take more than a momentary interest in her legs never seemed to come about. Her legs continued to produce an effect neither elegant nor exciting. Men merely passed her in the street as if she were some sort of female crank. This went on for several weeks until one perishingly cold rainy morning she was slightly late for her train, found every second class seat filled and was obliged to travel first.

The only other person in the carriage was a man of about her own age and it immediately struck her that he too had dressed in a hurry. One half of his blue necktie was inside his shirt collar and the other half outside. This aroused in her a strong and growing desire not only to tell him of the fact but also to get up and re-arrange the tie nearer, as it were, to her heart's desire.

While this feeling mounted she kept crossing and uncrossing her legs, revealing a blue-stockinged knee for a few minutes and then a green one for a time. All the while she tried reading her *Times* and then, finding herself unable to concentrate, put it down on the seat beside her.

About a minute later the man coughed, leaned forward and said with great politeness :

'I wonder if I might borrow your *Times?* I couldn't get one myself.'

'Oh! certainly. Certainly. By all means.'

'It's most awfully kind of you.'

Miss Stratton gave a polite smile and handed over *The Times.* In the instant before the man lifted up the paper to begin reading it she caught another glimpse of the blue necktie protruding from under its collar and she felt she knew, with certainty, that the man was unmarried. No woman would ever have let a man out of the house, she was sure, with collar and tie so painfully dishevelled.

As she pondered on this thought, at the same time wondering if she dared mention the curious state of the necktie, she stared out of the window, watching the black bare winter landscape slipping past, every field rain-soaked under a sky of driving cloud.

When she turned her glance to the man again it was to be confronted with an immense surprise. At first she found it impossible to believe what she saw. Then a second, third and finally a prolonged fourth look convinced her that she wasn't dreaming.

The man was reading *The Times* completely upside down.

'The necktie,' she told herself, 'I can understand. That's just a slip in the hurry of getting ready. Like my stockings. Anyone could do a thing like that. But reading the paper upside down – that simply can't be an accident. That simply can't be.'

At once it seemed to her imperative that she must do something about this curious state of affairs and she suddenly leaned forward and said :

'Oh! excuse me.'

'Yes?'

'I hope – I don't know if you know, but you're reading *The Times* upside down.'

'Yes, I do know.'

Miss Stratton sat open-mouthed, too flabbergasted to speak.

'Yes, I do know. I prefer it that way.'

'You actually – you mean – but isn't it frightfully difficult?'

'Not at all. I've been doing it for years.'

'But isn't it a strain? Wouldn't it be easier the right way up?'

'It's more fun this way. Besides I've got used to it.' He gave a quick shy smile, a gesture that struck her as being rather squirrel-like. 'I've been doing it ever since I was a boy. I got awfully interested in codes and that sort of thing. You know how boys are – turning words round, dropping letters, making X stand for one vowel and Y for another. I started to write sentences backwards and then of course it was only another step to reading things upside down.'

Again Miss Stratton was too surprised to speak.

'Have a try yourself.' The man held out *The Times* to her. 'It's extraordinarily easy once you – it's really a simple matter of concentration.'

'Oh! I don't think I could possibly –'

'Try.'

Suddenly Miss Stratton was aware of the man sitting next to her. They were holding *The Times* together, upside down.

'Try the headline. This one.'

Miss Stratton stared for fully half a minute at the paper, eyes groping behind her smoky-rose spectacles, like a child trying to read for the first time.

'I simply can't make head or tail of it. It looks sort of like Russian.'

'Oh! it's easy. It says *U.S. Lose More Helicopters in Vietnam. Vietcong Casualties Reported Heavy.*'

'Oh! so it does. I see now. I must be very stupid.'

'Not at all. It just needs practice.' The man gave a short treble laugh that Miss Stratton found most engaging. It struck her as being quite boyish. 'The curious part is that when you've been reading upside down for ages it seems most odd when you start reading right way up.'

'Yes, I suppose *that* could happen.'

'It's all a question of viewpoint. After all the world's pretty well upside down as it is, wouldn't you think?'

Miss Stratton laughed too and said she would indeed.

'You know,' he suddenly went on, 'but you're the first person who's ever drawn my attention to the fact that I read upside down. Hundreds of people every year see me doing it in the train but not one has ever said a word. I suppose they're either too shy or they think I'm mad. Do you think I'm mad?'

'Oh! not at all. Not at all.'

'It's merely a question of reversing convention –'

'Can you do it with figures?'

'Oh! with figures, yes. I can add up backwards and so on – it's a mental exercise, you see. A challenge.'

For some five minutes or more the train had been running slowly. With slight irritation the man took his watch from his waistcoat pocket – it hung from a thin gold chain – and looked at it.

'Thought so. Running late again. It's a confounded nuisance, this line. Every day last week we were late by ten minutes or more.'

'The evening trains are worse.'

'I know. Which one do you catch? The 6.10?'

Yes, she always caught the 6.10, Miss Stratton said. In fact she invariably caught the 5.20.

'I don't think I've ever run across you before, have I?' He looked quickly down at Miss Stratton's legs, encased as they always were in odd stockings, one green and one blue. 'I'm sure I'd remember if I had.'

Miss Stratton felt herself flush very slightly, without a word to say.

'I used to come on the 5.20,' he said, 'but the thing was a madhouse. A terrible bun-fight.'

'I think it's because I usually travel second that you haven't seen me.'

'Ah! possibly, possibly.'

Again he took a quick hard look at Miss Stratton's stockings. The matter of the stockings struck him as being no less unusual than Miss Stratton found his reading *The Times* upside down. Why did a woman go to work in stockings that didn't match? Most curious. You might well think her mad.

'I always stop off across the road at Porter's Wine Bar for a sherry,' he said. 'I allow myself that bit of extra time. It's a good relaxer. You wouldn't care to join me, I suppose, this evening?'

Totally ignorant of what prompted her to say so Miss Stratton suddenly said she really didn't know. It all depended on her friend.

'Oh! I see.'

Miss Stratton, who had invented the friend on the spur of the moment purely because she was rather flummoxed, now found herself trapped with the problem of getting rid of the friend.

'Well, perhaps some other evening. By the way my name's Fletcher.'

'It's very nice of you, Mr Fletcher. I daresay I could phone my friend.'

'Oh! could you? That would be nice. The sherry's awfully good at this place. Of course one can have something else. A glass of burgundy. They have champagne by the glass too.'

As he said this Miss Stratton found herself unaccountably inspired to laughter.

'I suppose,' she said, 'you don't by any chance drink upside down too?'

'That's a thought,' Mr Fletcher said and was unaccountably inspired to laughter too.

That evening, on the 6.10 train, Miss Stratton found herself deeply flushed and panting as she flopped into the corner of the first carriage, with Mr Fletcher opposite her. The fact that they had had to run for the train, together with two large glasses of sherry – they were called schooners, Mr Fletcher informed her – occasionally made her giggle briefly as she sought to recover breath.

'Well, that was a close-run thing,' Mr Fletcher said. 'Still, if we'd missed it we'd have had an excuse for another schooner.'

'Oh! those schooners. They must be trebles.'

Having finally got his breath back too Mr Fletcher took a rapid glance at Miss Stratton's legs, only to find a further interesting surprise awaiting him there. During her lunch hour, in a sudden upremeditated rush of abandon, Miss Stratton had brought herself some new stockings and was now wearing one of a bright raspberry rose and another of a shade of muted violet. They contrasted and yet blended very well, she thought.

Mr Fletcher was impelled to think so too but was far too shy to look at them for more than a few seconds or to say so.

He really wanted to say something else but it was only after reading his evening paper upside down for another half hour that he at last found courage enough to do so.

'Do you know this place, Purland Court?' he said. 'They've turned it into flats.'

No, Miss Stratton said, she didn't think she did.

'It used to be the old Bradfield house. Big Victorian thing, in its own park. I've got one of the flats. Oh! it's only one of the very small ones. Right at the top. A maid's box room originally, I suppose.'

'It's not the place with the huge wrought iron gates?'

'That's it. Marvellously beautiful in spring. Big avenue of limes with millions and millions of aconites blooming underneath. As early as February. All gold.'

'What are aconites? I'm afraid I'm awfully bad about flowers.'

Mr Fletcher explained about aconites and how he loved them. To him, he didn't know why, they represented something Grecian. They brought spring into winter, he said, and as he spoke of them Miss Stratton was touched into thinking that his voice took on a certain urgent but at the same time bemused note of tenderness.

'Will you be on the train tomorrow?' he finally said.

'Oh! I'm on it every day,' Miss Stratton again found herself briefly giggling. 'Always on the treadmill.'

'I'll look out for you. Perhaps we could indulge in another schooner.'

Something about the word indulge instantly illuminated the otherwise drab atmosphere of the railway carriage. There was something intimate and warm about it too: a feeling that almost brought Miss Stratton to the point of saying something about Mr Fletcher's necktie, which had evidently remained half in, half outside his collar all day. Instead she merely gazed at it with her own air of bemusement. And then Mr Fletcher said:

'Just in case I miss you in the morning shall we say we'll meet in the wine bar at half past five? That is unless you have to see your friend.'

Oh! she didn't think she had to see her friend tomorrow, said Miss Stratton, now under the vexatious impression that Mr Fletcher understood her friend to be a man.

'Oh! Good.' Mr Fletcher gave her a shy smile and went on to say how pleasant it had all been, meeting her and the sherry and everything.

Miss Stratton said it had been pleasant too and finally went home to an early bed, where for some considerable time she sat reading her newspaper upside down, an experience that troubled her so much that she afterwards didn't sleep well.

The next morning Mr Fletcher arrived on the train with a small posy of fifteen or twenty yellow aconites wrapped in tissue paper. Miss Stratton, amazed that flowers of such delicacy, and so Grecian in feeling, as Mr Fletcher maintained, could produce their cool fresh beauty in the darkest hours of winter, kept them all day, and then for the rest of the week, on her office desk, in a small blue plastic tumbler.

Every time she gazed at them she saw Mr Fletcher's necktie, the knot of which, that morning, was somewhere in the region of his left ear.

After that they started to meet every evening in the wine bar, religiously repeating the ritual of indulging in schooners. Each evening too Miss Stratton went home to read her newspaper upside down, thereby experiencing a curious intimate thrill, almost as if Mr Fletcher were in bed with her.

All this might have gone on quite uninterrupted if Miss Stratton hadn't happened to remark one evening 'Oh! I don't see my friend now – I – well, let's not talk about it.'

Mr Fletcher seemed to think this at last released him from some obligation or other and after some minutes of apparent contemplation said:

'I've been wondering if you might care to come and see my little place sometime. It's very modest, but –'

'Oh! I should love to.'

'You couldn't by some remote chance come to lunch? Say on Sunday.'

Miss Stratton said she would be quite absolutely delighted and immediately started to wonder what she would wear. For several days she went on wondering, finally coming to the conclusion that since Mr Fletcher lived in a flat in a Victorian mansion she had better dress accordingly. As a result she bought herself an entirely new outfit, a two piece linen suit in pale green that made her look unusually neat, even a little elegant.

She also decided to discard, for once, the odd stockings and instead wore perfectly ordinary nylons in a flesh-pink shade.

'The trouble is there's no lift. I do hope you're not completely fagged out, climbing the stairs.'

Miss Stratton, more than a little flustered after climbing four flights of stairs, the last narrow and very steep, eventually found herself contemplating the crazy cell of what Mr Fletcher called his little place. A gas-stove piled with books, a divan bed on which slept three white cats, a bicycle draped with bundles of dried beech leaves, a sewing machine of the old treadle kind on which stood plates, wine-glasses, and bottles of tomato ketchup, a bowl of bananas and custard and an unopened tin of sardines, a bureau littered with a mass of papers, some of them held down with pots of crocuses, others with pots of jam, jars of fish paste and even, in one instance, a half eaten currant loaf: the whole appeared to her to have come out of some lunatic dream. She was also strongly aware of an odour of stale fish combined with the sort of dusty pungency that comes of floors long unswept and windows long unopened.

'I'm afraid I'm a bit tucked for space,' Mr Fletcher said.

Quite unable to make any sort of comment on this, Miss Stratton found herself mournfully distressed for Mr Fletcher, who was also attired to match the shabby confusion of his little place. His clothes, consisting of a pair of flabby plus-fours the colour of horse manure and a polo-necked sweater that appeared to have been dipped in a solution of stale beer and axle grease, threw her own new pale green suit into such relief that she was now almost ashamed for having put it on.

While Mr Fletcher poured out sherry into a pair of chipped tooth-glasses Miss Stratton could only wonder what lunch was going to consist of. Mr Fletcher soon informed her:

'I did knock up a pigeon and steak pie. I normally do it rather well. But I went into the park to look for primroses and left the gas too high and the thing burnt to a cinder. I hope you don't mind sardines? They ought to marry fairly well with the wine.'

71

Jammed between gas-stove and bureau was a low couch, from which Mr Fletcher presently removed a basket of swede turnips, a portable radio, two empty sherry bottles, a shooting bag and a box of gramophone records, so that he and Miss Stratton could sit down.

'These are the first primroses. They're very early this year. I wanted awfully to get a few to put on the lunch table.'

The primroses were in an egg-cup. Miss Stratton again mournfully touched, held them to her face, breathing in the delicate velvet scent of them.

'I always think you get the whole of spring in the scent of primroses,' Mr Fletcher said. 'It takes you back through all the springs of your life.'

Such remarks of Mr Fletcher's always affected her deeply. It was almost as if Mr Fletcher had stroked her hand or put his face against hers. They had an intolerable, elusive intimacy.

In the intervals of pouring and drinking sherry Mr Fletcher got up to cut thick slices of brown bread and butter. Miss Stratton, wondering continually about the lunch table, of which she could so far see no sign, was prompted to ask if she could by any chance help?

'I generally eat on the sewing machine,' Mr Fletcher said. 'The thing folds in and you get a flat top. It's about right for two.'

'Shall I arrange it a bit?'

'Oh! would you? That's awfully nice of you.'

Miss Stratton did her best to arrange the lunch table. The plain white tablecloth, much creased, had several holes in it and these she covered with pepper and salt pots, plates and the bowl of bananas and custard. While she was doing this Mr Fletcher opened the tin of sardines and said:

'I rather fancy the sardines should be good. They're very old. Did you know that sardines improved with age? Like wine?'

Miss Stratton said no, she wasn't aware of that. She herself had no great fondness for sardines, though she was too embarrassed to say so, and now secretly wondered if Mr Fletcher wouldn't allow her to poach some eggs or make an omelette or something of that sort.

Emboldened by a third glass of sherry, she at last made up her mind to suggest this. It would be the easiest thing in the world. And which did he prefer? Poached eggs or omelette?

'I adore omelettes actually.'

Very well, Miss Stratton said, she would do omelettes. She in fact rather prided herself on her omelettes. Had Mr Fletcher any sort of thing to flavour them with? Cheese or ham or something?

'I've got a tin of mushrooms somewhere,' Mr Fletcher said and started to search for them in the jungle of his little place, eventually finding them in the bureau, mixed up with tins of cat food.

'I know it's the right one,' Mr Fletcher said, 'because it's the one without the label.'

Miss Stratton, at once revolted by the thought of cat food, profoundly hoped it was. In the end it proved to be and Miss Stratton proceeded to make the omelette, the excellence of which Mr Fletcher praised with a typically shy enthusiasm throughout the meal.

After lunch Mr Fletcher sat on the couch and read the Sunday newspapers upside down. Once he looked up to see Miss Stratton reading hers upside down too and said:

'I see you're getting the knack of it. It really isn't all that difficult, is it?'

No, Miss Stratton said, it wasn't, and then caught Mr Fletcher in the act of gazing at her knees, above which her skirt had ridden up some inches. She hoped that this might mean that Mr Fletcher was taking a greater and more intimate interest in her legs and that in consequence he might suggest that she sat on the sofa with him. But nothing of the kind happened at all.

During subsequent weeks nothing happened either. Mr Fletcher was always kind, polite, considerate, attentive, anxious to please. On the train he brought Miss Stratton little nosegays of violets, once a bunch of cowslips, a pot of white cyclamen for her office desk and in due course a bunch of roses. In the evenings they drank sherry together. On Sundays she cooked lunch for him among the shambles of the sewing machine, the cats, the strewn papers and the clinging odour of fish.

But of the things she wanted most there was no sign. She longed for Mr Fletcher to make a gesture of something more than mere friendship: to touch her knee, to rest his face against hers, to make a gesture of affection, even love. At night, alone in bed, she even entertained the wild notion that one day Mr Fletcher might suddenly lose his head and kiss her, even approach her with passion. In such moods she was always ready to surrender.

But by midsummer nothing had happened; and Miss Stratton, half in despair, at last decided to do something about it.

She decided to re-introduce her friend.

Her friend, she reasoned, might arouse in Mr Fletcher a keener interest in herself, even jealousy.

'Well, I'm awfully afraid I can't meet you tonight. You see, my friend –'

Curiously enough her increasing refusals had on Mr Fletcher an effect quite opposite from that she hoped and intended. Far from becoming more attentive, passionate or even jealous, Mr Fletcher became more and more depressed, turning more and more in upon himself, painfully spurned. Finally, on a hot, humid Sunday in July, they quarrelled.

An unexpectedly prolonged beautiful spell of weather had inspired Mr Fletcher to suggest a picnic in the park. At this time of year the long avenue of limes was in full flower: a great heavenly cathedral of perfume, the whole essence of summer.

Mr Fletcher had suggested one o'clock for the picnic but it was in fact past two o'clock when Miss Stratton arrived. When Mr Fletcher uttered some mild remonstrance about this, slightly agitated that some accident might have befallen her, she said:

'Well, I had a phone call from my friend – I couldn't very well not talk –'

In addition to being deliberately late Miss Stratton had also bought herself a new summer dress: a pale yellow short-sleeved shantung, purposely low at the neck. She had been inspired to do this by reading an article in a magazine which had examined the age-old causes of the things by which women attracted men. It seemed that the mode of attraction by the exposure of the legs was comparatively recent; until modern times the legs had been scrupulously concealed. The bosom, on the other hand, especially in the 18th century, had long been exposed.

She and Mr Fletcher sat in the shade of a huge old limetree to eat a picnic of ham, green salad, cheese, tomatoes and finally strawberries and cream, together with a bottle of white Alsatian wine. The scent of limes drenching the air was heavy and exotic. The taste of the wine, flowery too, matched it perfectly.

After the strawberries and cream Miss Stratton lay back on the grass, legs carelessly exposed, the slightest curve of her bosom faintly revealed. Now and then she gave a replete, indulgent sigh, breathing in the scent of limes with a sound that expressed a sleepy, dreamy, ecstasy. All Mr Fletcher did in response was to read his newspaper upside down.

'Must you read your newspaper?'

'Well, I always do. There isn't much point in having one if one doesn't read it.'

'This heavenly day and all you can think of is to bury your head in a lot of stocks and shares or something.'

'Well, I'm sorry. Of course if it offends you –'

'I didn't say it offended me. I said this heavenly day and all you can do is to turn into a book-worm – a newspaper-worm – or something.'

'I don't think I care for the word worm. Whatever's come over you?'

'Nothing has come over me, as you fondly put it.'

'You shock me. I've never heard you speak like this.'

For some minutes Miss Stratton lay grimly, resolutely silent. Then she suddenly uttered a peremptory, whispered 'My God!'

'And what, pray, was that in aid of?' Mr Fletcher said.

'Oh! read your wretched newspaper!'

'Really.'

Miss Stratton, silent and impotent, stared up through the great canopy of leaves and keys of lime flower above her head. Only the minutest fragments of sky, like segments of bright blue broken glass, were visible beyond.

'What am I expected to do?' Mr Fletcher said.

'Do? Well, you could admire my new dress, for one thing. Or even notice it.'

'I have noticed it. I like it.'

'Like it! My friend went into raptures about it.'

'Am I to take it that you'd rather be with your friend?'

'I didn't say that. All I said was – Oh! never mind.'

For more than another half hour they were completely silent. Once Miss Stratton, as if half-suffocated by the drenching heat of afternoon, loosened still further the neck of her dress and wiped the damp upper curves of her neck and bosom with a handkerchief.

At last Mr Fletcher said in a flat, almost morbid monotone:

'We seem to have wasted a whole afternoon.'

'We!' Miss Stratton could bear it no longer and suddenly sprang to her feet. 'We, for Heaven's sake! Include me out, as they say.'

'Oh! my dear, I never thought we'd come to this.'

'Don't "my dear" me!'

To Mr Fletcher's utter astonishment Miss Stratton was already walking away.

'Where on earth are you going?'

'Going? Where do you think I'm going? I'm going to see my friend. Note the word. Friend – friend!'

Head high in the air, under the blazing July sun, Miss Stratton stormed away across the park.

For nearly two months after this she never saw Mr Fletcher on the train. Nor did she ever see him in the wine bar, where she sometimes lingered in the evenings, sipping sherry and hoping that by some sort of miracle he might appear.

Finally, unable to bear it any longer, she went over to Mr Fletcher's flat, his little place. She climbed the long flights of stairs, knocked several times on the door and also rang the bell, without getting an answer. As she then came down again a woman appeared from a flat below and said :

'Was there something I could do to help you?'

'I was looking for Mr Fletcher.'

'Oh! Mr Fletcher doesn't live here now.'

'No?'

'He took a flat in London. Said he found the train journey every day very tiresome.'

'You don't know the address?'

'I'm afraid not. He went off awfully suddenly. We all thought he looked ill. The stairs seemed to be too much for him. You'd hear him positively fighting for breath. In the way asthmatics do.'

'Was he asthmatic?'

'Oh! pitifully. I thought he'd die once or twice. In fact I'm ashamed to say it but I watch the obituary columns every day – it's a dreadful thought, I know, but I wouldn't want to miss it.'

Miss Stratton started to watch the obituary columns too. Almost a year later she read that Mr Fletcher, who always read his newspaper upside down and could only express himself to her in such simple things as aconites, a bunch of primroses, a glass of sherry or a rose or two, had died.

Miss Stratton is now married to a man named Rawlinson, who has a wholesale business in paints, emulsions and materials of that sort. They live in a villa furnished down to the smallest, correctest detail by a firm of decorators; the garden too has been landscaped for them and has a professional, orderly, impeccable, shorn and bloodless air.

Rawlinson is a man of intensely scrupulous habits who gets

up at half past six every morning in order to complete a holy ritual of shaving, clipping his moustache, oiling his hair, anointing himself with after-shave lotions, brushing his teeth and manicuring his neat shell-like nails in order to be at his desk punctually on the stroke of nine. Every day he lunches at his office. Every evening he goes home at nine o'clock to find the former Miss Stratton playing patience or knitting or reading or watching television, waiting for supper. When he is away from home, however far away, his office telephones him twice a day with the day's figures, orders and events in minutest detail. When he dines out he peruses, rather than reads, the menu with the same fine incisive attention to every single item, as if it were as sacred as holy writ.

His behaviour to the former Miss Stratton is equally scrupulous, impeccable, orderly and correct. He flatters himself that she has everything she could possibly wish for. There is nothing she lacks.

Sometimes, in the middle of this secure and well-ordered world, Miss Stratton thinks of Mr Fletcher and such small things as his aconites, his primroses and his sherry; and sometimes, when alone or when Rawlinson isn't looking, she also reads her newspaper upside down.

It is only then that the world seems to her to be right way up and she can view it with a better understanding.

How Vainly Men Themselves Amaze

THE sand on the seaward side of the dunes glittered like fine white sugar in the sun. A plastic ball, in white and yellow stripes, rolled softly and with deceptive slowness from one dry tuft of dune-grass to another, not at all unlike a big bored snail, until suddenly a sharper gust of breeze caught it and tossed it bouncing high across the shore.

For the third time that morning young Franklin raced after it, retrieved it and took it back to the auburn-haired woman in the two piece emerald swim-suit sitting at the foot of the dunes. For the third time too she waved her orange-pink nails in the air in protest, smiling with lips of the same colour at the same time.

'Oh! this is becoming an awful bore for you. It really is. Thank you all the same – it's awfully sweet of you – but next time just let it go.'

'That's all right – I'm not doing anything –'

'Can you see those children of mine anywhere or that wretched German girl? She's supposed to look after the ball.'

'I think I saw them going that way, towards the pines. I think they were gathering shells.'

'Anything useless, of course. That's these girls all over. Anything useless.'

He stood looking down at her, feeling slightly awkward, still holding the ball in his hands. She was a beautifully boned woman, about forty, evenly tanned to a deep gold, her stomach flat, her navel a delicate shadowy shell. Beside her on the sand stood a straw basket stuffed with a pink towel, a pair of yellow beach shoes and a yellow scarf, together with a second flatter basket of bananas, peaches and pears. With her long orange-pink finger tips she patted the sand beside her and said :

'May I offer you some fruit? I feel I somehow ought to

reward you for all your tiresome dashing up and down. Anyway, sit down, won't you?'

He hesitated, awkward again, not knowing what to do with the ball.

'Oh! let the wretched ball go. It's a confounded nuisance. I feel I never want to see it again.'

He looked up and down the dunes and then said :

'I'll drop it in this hollow here. It probably won't blow out of there –'

'Oh! let it go.'

He laid the ball in a deep nest of grass, tossing sand round it. She waited for him to finish and then, as he was about to sit down, said :

'Oh! before you sit down would you be an absolute dear and do something for me?'

'Of course, if I can.'

'Go as far as the kiosk and get me a bottle of milk, would you? It's all I ever have for lunch, just milk and fruit.'

Like an over-obedient servant he turned swiftly on his heels, ready to run.

'No, no, wait. Here's some francs. And wouldn't you like to get yourself something too? A beer or something? or would it spoil your lunch?'

'Oh! I never go back to the hotel for lunch. I always grab a sandwich or something down here.'

'Well, bring yourself something anyway. Just what you like. I never go back either. The children and Heidi go back, thank God. That gets them out of my sight.'

When he came back, five minutes later, carrying a bottle of milk, two bottles of beer and four ham rolls, she was lying flat on her stomach, her long beautifully shaped legs stretched straight out, the soles of her feet flat. Something about the pure crinkled whiteness of the underside of her feet stirred him sharply and held him for some moments almost hypnotized.

Suddenly she turned over and saw him staring down at them. For an instant he half flushed as if she had caught him in the act of doing something indiscreet and then she sat up and said:

'Oh! that was awfully quick. I didn't expect you back for ages.'

'I bought myself some beer and ham rolls. I hope that's all right?'

'Of course. I expect you're ravenous.'

Innumerable small sugary grains of sand clung to her arms and thighs, the two pieces of her swim-suit and the upper part of her breasts. As she brushed them away with her hands and even, once, dipped a hand down between her breasts she said that that was the worst of sand. It got into everything. He must be careful it didn't get into his sandwiches.

He sat down, putting the bottle of milk and the two beer bottles on the sand.

'Oh! damn, I forgot about an opener.'

'Don't worry. I'm well equipped. I've got everything.'

By now it was midday and with a miraculous swiftness the shore began to empty itself of people. Everywhere French families were hastily drying bodies, packing up belongings, drifting away.

'You don't see that wretched girl and the children coming back, do you? No, they've probably gone the other way. We're at the *Angleterre*. Where are you?'

'*Les Salles d'Or*.'

'By yourself?'

'With my parents.'

Suddenly she waved her long fingers and asked him to look at the beach. The French were really extraordinary creatures of habit. Dead on the stroke of twelve the beach emptied every day. You'd think a plague had struck it or something. It was all nonsense about the French being so slap-happy and fast and loose and so on. They were really immensely conventional. Didn't he think so? Did he like France anyway?

'It bores me a bit.'

For the first time she looked at him with absolute directness and for the first time he became acutely aware of the peculiar nature of her eyes. The pupils of them were like bright birds' eggs, mottled and stencilled green and orange-brown. For fully a quarter of a minute she held him in a gaze without the flicker of an eyelid and then at last said :

'Good. That makes two of us.'

Sharply disturbed, he lowered his own gaze and too hastily started to open a bottle of beer. It frothed violently, spilling down his thighs.

'Here. Here's a tissue,' she said and before he could take it wiped the beer away herself with long smooth strokes.

His body gave a quick central stir. His blood seemed to curdle in the hot bristling Atlantic air and he took a swift drink of beer. As if totally unaware that anything had remotely disturbed him she took a red plastic beaker from her basket and poured it full of milk. The sight of the milk shining pinkly through the plastic and then of her orange-pink mouth held against the lip of the beaker convulsed his body still more sharply, for the second time.

'You haven't told me your name.'

'Franklin. Everybody calls me Frankie.'

'Why does France bore you?'

He drank at the beer again and said he didn't really know. He supposed it might be his parents. They were rather elderly and mad keen on gastronomique excursions, trying new places to eat, new dishes and that sort of thing. That bored him; well, anyway, too much of it. He was perfectly happy with a beer and a sandwich and plenty of swimming.

'You've got magnificently brown, I must say.'

'You too. You're a marvellous colour.'

'Well, it's an art. I take it gently. Not too long at a time. I shall lie in the shade this afternoon.'

He started to eat a ham roll, washing it down with an occasional drink of beer. She, using a small silver knife, began to peel a peach, taking off the thin rose downy skin with delicate strokes and then carefully, almost meticulously, laying the fragments on another paper tissue. When finally she bit into the ripe flesh of the peach he saw for the first time how full her lips were. In contrast to the fine whiteness of her teeth and the green creaminess of the peach they shone richly and as peach-juice ran over them and she licked it away the slow curl of her tongue was voluptuous.

'I adore these peaches,' she started to say and then suddenly broke off, a look of stiff annoyance on her face. At the same time he caught the sound of children's voices and looked round to see, thirty yards away, a small boy and a girl and a blonde tall young woman in a plain white swimsuit and carrying a blue wrap, coming across the shore. Even at that distance he thought the girl had an aloof aristocratic, even supercilious air.

The boy, in nothing but a pair of short blue swim-trunks, came running in great excitement.

'We had smashing fun. We found an old anchor – it had barnacles stuck all over it – and an old rope and a big crab. I wanted to bring the crab but Heidi and June said it was too dead –'

'All right, darling, all right. Off you go now to lunch.' She turned sharply to the tall German girl. The mottled green-brown eyes held the pale blue almost transparent eyes of the girl in a stare of tense and unconcealed dislike. In return the frigid blue eyes were motionless, calm and equally hostile. 'I thought I always told you to get the children back by twelve. It's long past that now. You know how those French wolves raid the *salle à manger*.'

'Yes, Mrs Palgrave. But sometimes there is a moment when children are too happy to be –'

'Oh! buzz along. And take that silly ball with you. It's been plaguing us to death all morning.'

'I'll get it,' Franklin said and leapt to his feet, beer bottle in hand, and ran to get the ball.

When he eventually brought it to the German girl she looked first at him and then at the beer, at the same time smiling with totally unexpected friendliness. It at once struck him that her hair was almost identical in colour with the sand, so incredibly fine and sun-bleached that it was almost white.

She took the ball from him and said: 'Thank you. Your beer looks good. It makes me thirsty.'

'Oh! wouldn't you have some? There's another bottle –'

'Oh! don't start pampering her. Run along, Heidi. June's already half way there.'

The German girl gave him a final quick, almost confidential smile, and then walked away. The boy called *'Au revoir! Good-bye!'* and ran ahead of her in jumping spirals of excitement and then suddenly, remembering his duty, came running back to kiss his mother.

'Oh! Go away. Your hands are simply filthy. You'd better wash well before you go into lunch. You smell of that beastly crab. Heidi! – see that he washes! –'

In ten seconds the harshness of this episode had melted away. With an amazement touched by embarrassment he saw the expression on her face miraculously transformed, all tension gone. She resumed the business of sucking at the peach as if nothing had happened, the mottled eyes warm with reflected sea-light.

'These girls are an awful responsibility,' she said, but quietly and without rancour. 'I sometimes wonder what she does on her days off. It quite scares me. She looks cold-blooded enough, but you never know, underneath. How did she strike you? – I mean, as a man?'

He laughed quickly. 'Man – well, eighteen. Yes, I suppose so.'

'Eighteen? Good gracious, you look twenty-three or more.' She gave him a bland, unequivocal stare of admiration, eyes immobile and precisely focussed. 'Well, how *did* she strike you? or are you not one of those who size people up very quickly?'

'No, I don't think I do. At first I thought she looked terribly supercilious and then – I don't know –'

'I'm afraid I'm the impetuous sort. Sum people up at first sight – twinkling of an eye sort of thing. I'm not often wrong either. You, for instance –'

'How do you mean, me?'

By now she had finished the peach and was engaged in peeling, with the same delicacy, a long gold-green pear. Before answering she peeled off a long curl of skin and took a slow drink of milk.

'Well, now, tell me if I'm wrong. Generous – sensitive – not malicious, not in the least – perhaps a bit impetuous, like me, or anyway eager to please. And, what's getting rare these days, nice manners.'

'Gosh, I'd never measure up to that lot.'

'Oh! don't be modest.' She smiled at him once again with such fixed and candid warmth that he felt his body convulse almost violently. 'Of course you do.'

He gnawed at his third ham roll and drank more beer, not knowing what to say.

'I suppose you've left school? or have you?'

'Last term.'

'And now what are you going to do?'

'Photography. I hope.'

She said that was interesting and sliced the pear in half and then scooped out the cores, leaving the hollows half-filled with juice. This too ran down her chin as she ate the pear and once again she licked it away voluptuously.

'I didn't bring my camera down this morning. First time for days. Stupid of me – I'd awfully like to take a picture of you.'

'Oh! would you? That's nice.'

'Would you mind? I could easily go back and get it after lunch. I've got one of those jobs that takes dozens. You could pick out the ones you liked best and I'd have them blown up.'

'You see. I was right. I said you were generous.'

Half an hour later he got up to go back to the hotel to fetch his camera. In the moment before he walked away she said:

'By the time you get back I'll have retreated to the pines. I've had my ration of sun for the day. You'll find me in the shade.'

By the time he had fetched his camera it was nearly half past two. All across the sand gay coloured umbrellas were going up in the sun; the shore was filling with people.

Just as he reached the sand he heard a shrill voice saying 'I'm going to play with the crab again' and turned to see the German girl and the two children a dozen yards away. The boy said 'Heidi, look, that's the man who was talking to Mummy.' Franklin stopped and waited and said 'Hullo' and the German girl gave him a short, rather frigid smile without a word of greeting.

It suddenly struck him then that what he thought to be superciliousness was perhaps, after all, mere shyness. The effect on him was to make him feel slightly shy and awkward too and in order to counteract it he said to the boy :

'Did you wash?'

'Oh! yes, he washed,' she said. 'I saw to that.'

'Good. Now I can take your picture.' He smiled at the German girl, who promptly dropped the illustrated magazine she was carrying. He picked it up with equal promptitude, dashed sand from it and said : 'Perhaps I could take yours too?'

'Yes, of course. Are you keen on photography?'

'Very. I hope to take it up. I mean professionally. For a living.'

Back at the hotel he had slipped on a white rowing blazer and from one of the pockets he now took out his light exposure meter. The boy at once wanted to know what this was and Franklin jocularly said it was a gadget for measuring whether little boys were telling the truth or not. The joke was lost on the boy but the German girl immediately laughed with such spontaneity, her mouth wide open, her head thrown back, that everything about her was suddenly and amazedly warm. The transformation was so startling that he laughed infectiously too and in a second of quick inspiration lifted the camera to his eye.

'That ought to be a beauty.'

'More probably I shall look an awful sight.'

'Oh! no, you couldn't possibly do that.'

At once her face was cool again, the shyness back. He too

felt a moment of awkwardness and started to say that now he would take the three of them together, but to his surprise he suddenly realized that the boy's sister was no longer with them.

'I didn't see her go. Where on earth –'

'Oh! I have my eye on her. She's right over there, by the sea. It's very typical of her – she's what you call contrary in English – independent. Still, I'd better go after her before she goes too far – it's more than my life's worth –'

'Just one more before you go – may I?'

'I think it better I go. We shall see each other again perhaps?'

'I'm sure – I hope so.'

A moment later she and the boy were running across the sand. Looking after them he found the glitter of light on the sea almost painful to his eyes. He took a pair of sun-glasses from his pocket and put them on and then started to walk slowly away in the opposite direction, towards the pines.

In the shade of the pines, as she had said she would be, Mrs Palgrave was lying flat on her back, her long elegant legs looking for some reason even more golden in shadow than in sun.

'Oh! there you are. I hardly recognized you in that smart white blazer and the dark glasses. You seem to have been gone an awful long time.'

He took off the sun-glasses and sat down on the pine-needled sand beside her.

'I ran into the children and the German girl. That's why.'

'Oh! you did?'

'I think I got a good picture of Heidi. A real beauty.'

'Indeed.'

The air under the trees, thick with pine odour, seemed oppressive. He started to take off his blazer and she watched him in silence for some moments before saying :

'Would you be an awful dear and let me use that as a pillow? Would you mind? The sand isn't so soft here.'

'Of course, of course –'

With great eagerness he started to fold up the blazer.

'Just tuck it under my head, will you? I feel terribly lazy – I suppose it's the warm afternoon.'

He knelt down and she half lifted her head, drowsily. Then he put one hand under the thick red mass of her hair and lifted her head still higher and slipped the folded blazer underneath it.

'That's lovely. That's nice. Thank you.'

She gave a sleepy sinuous movement with her body, closed her eyes for a fraction of a second and then opened them again to smile at him with slow bemusement.

'What's the blazer for? Tennis?'

'Rowing.'

'That makes the muscles strong, I know.'

She gave his right forearm a sudden compulsive grip and he said:

'Careful with that. I broke it a year ago.'

She gave him another slow smile that lingered for some moments somewhere between teasing and mockery and then said:

'How did you come to do that? Resisting some terrible Amazon or something of that sort?'

'No. Quite simple. I was just skating.'

She patted the forearm quickly and then withdrew her hand.

'What sort of boat do you row in?'

'An eight. Or did, rather. I had to give it up because of the arm.'

'Did you win lots of marvellous races?'

'A few. We got a third in the Head of the River once. On the Thames. Then we were going like stink on the Serpentine once, leading by three lengths, and then caught a crab.'

'A crab? Not the sort that wretched child of mine found this morning?'

'No, it's when a man gets his blade stuck in the water, sort of locked, and he can't get it out. There's nothing you can do about it. It stops the boat.'

'I'll bet it didn't happen to you.'

'I'm afraid it did. It can happen to anyone. You feel an awful damn fool.'

She suddenly let the conversation end, simply giving him another long, searching enigmatic smile.

At once he felt his body tighten like a bow string. He drew breath deeply, inhaling draughts of pine odour that were stronger, warmer, more oppressive than ever. On the white sand the red mass of her hair seemed to smoulder and as he stared down at it, fascinated to a point of intoxication, she asked him in the most casual of voices why he didn't come and lie down too? It was awfully, awfully comfortable.

In another moment he was lying side by side with her, looking close into her face. She gave the lightest of laughs and then slowly ran one hand across his bare shoulder. He moved his mouth rapidly to kiss her but she drew her face very slightly away, smiling and saying so this was the way he liked to amuse himself on warm –

She never finished the sentence. He suddenly smothered her mouth with his own. For fully a minute she lay there unresistant and it was only as his hands began to wander across her shoulders and then her breasts that she broke slightly free and said :

'And who gave you permission to do this sort of thing?'

'Do I need permission?'

'Well, at least an invitation.'

'Invite me –'

'You're invited.'

A moment later they were locked together and when finally they broke free again and his hand made a long caressive movement down the curve of her body there was only a single scalding thought in his mind.

'Not here,' she said, 'I don't think it's a good idea, here. I know a better place. Round the headland. A tiny bay about two miles down the coast. I go there sometimes – there's a bit more privacy – I've got the car –'

'Now shall we go?'

'Tomorrow. Don't rush things. I'm here all summer.'

'In the morning then?'

'Afternoon. I must have my ration of morning sun.' She gave her golden body a long still glance of self-admiration, slightly lifting her breasts. 'Don't tell me you don't think it's worth it? Sun in the morning. Love in the afternoon.'

After that, every afternoon, they drove down the coast, through pine forests, to where at last, like a small central bit taken out of an amber quarter moon of melon, a little bay lay within a bay. Dark rocks, like monolithic barriers, locked in a secret arena of sand not more than thirty yards wide, the roots of big pines grappling at the rock crests like claws of animals holding down stricken lumps of prey.

Here, in calmer moments, she coaxed him to talk more about himself. She on the other hand had little or nothing to say of herself and once when he started to question her she merely said 'Me? You don't want to know about me. Isn't it enough that I'm here?'

Every day he took many pictures of her, sometimes in the nude, sometimes in the sea, several times perched high on a rock, like some fabulous red-gold sea creature. She several times confessed that it gave her a strangely uncommon thrill to be photographed quite naked. It was something she'd never known before – it was like being watched by some secret eye.

From time to time he wondered if there could, possibly, be a Mr Palgrave, but there was no way of asking her this. Finally, as the secretive rapturous afternoons drew out to a number past counting he decided that it couldn't possibly matter about Mr Palgrave. Mr Palgrave was either divorced or dead, a faceless unhaunting shape somewhere far outside the world of sand and pines and sun and bristling salty air.

Then one afternoon she suddenly said:

'I'm afraid I'm going to have to leave you.'

At once his heart started bounding with shock. His throat choked thickly and he could barely manage to say:

'I thought you were here for the summer. You mean you're all going away?'

'Oh! good gracious, no. Only me. I've got to go back to London for a few days to see my solicitors. It's about a flat I'm buying. Papers to sign and all that.'

'Will you be gone very long?'

'At the outside three days.'

'God, I'll miss you.'

'I don't believe it. You're trying to flatter me. Out of sight out of mind. Anyway it'll do you good to have a rest from me. You can get sick even of love.'

'Not with you. I'll be bored to death again.'

Bored? Being bored, she told him with a teasing laugh, was merely like being hungry. When the excitement started again you ate it with so much better appetite. Ravenously. Even passionately.

But curiously, after she had gone, he found that he hardly missed her at all. All his emotions were exhausted, drained to a state of dry fatigue. In revulsion from passion he found that he wanted merely to swim, walk idly along the beach, read in the sun. What had been boredom now became a balm.

It wasn't until the early evening of the second day after Mrs Palgrave had left that he suddenly ran into Heidi and the two children as they crossed the shore. The day had been much hotter than usual, the air charged with a sharper exhausting saltiness, and he thought the children looked hot and tired.

'They're simply panting for iced drinks.'

'Me too. Let me treat you all. Will you? I feel I could drink beer by the gallon.'

By contrast to the children Heidi looked composed and cool. Under the shade of a big pink umbrella outside the kiosk her fair skin had the softest overtones of rose that gave her a more than usually friendly air, making him more than ever certain that her habitual aloofness arose merely from being shy.

'This orange is good,' she said. She rattled ice round and round in her long glass. 'They always make it of the real oranges here.' The children were drinking something of a lurid purple shade, capped with ice cream and dusted with flakes of chocolate.

'The beer's good too. It's awfully hot today.'

In less than five minutes all that remained in the children's glasses were smears of purplish cream.

'Another one, please, Heidi. More please. Heidi, be a pet.'

'A swim first. Then we'll see.'

When the children had gone off to the beach again she was very quiet for some moments, as if perhaps shy of being alone with him, and then she said :

'Mrs Palgrave has gone to London for a few days. Or perhaps you know?'

'Yes, I know.'

'I saw you with her several times.'

'Yes.'

At this she was very quiet again, her eyes lowered as she gently swished the ice round and round in her glass. He felt the silence to be of increasingly acute embarrassment and then realized that it was, after all, the first time they had been completely alone together.

'Oh! by the way, the picture I took of you came out very well. I haven't got it with me but I'll bring it next time I come down.'

'Thank you.'

Another and rather longer silence followed and he had just started to wonder if this might even be one of disapproval, as if perhaps she instinctively sensed how far his relationship with Mrs Palgrave might have gone, when he suddenly remembered that he had a question to ask her.

Was there a Mr Palgrave?

'Oh! yes, there is a Mr Palgrave.'

She took several slow sips of her orange juice, bending low over the glass, so that a strand or two of her extraordinarily fair hair fell across her face. She brushed them lightly back with her fingers and said :

'He is in some sort of business. I don't know what. In the city somewhere.'

'Does he ever come over?'

'Sometimes for a week-end. Every couple of weeks or so. He is always working.'

'What is he like?'

'He is rather older than she is. Rather a silent man.'

'A good old yes-and-no-type.'

'Yes, but rather more no than yes, I feel.'

The discussion of Mr Palgrave's virtues ended in another wall of silence. After several minutes Franklin finished his beer and then raised his hand to call the waiter for another. Would she perhaps like another orange juice at the same time?

'No, really, thank you.'

Before his second beer arrived he interrupted yet another silence to say :

'Would you mind very much if I asked you something?'

'Please ask.'

'Do you like fish?'

She actually broke into a high peal of laughter. He laughed too but was it really all that funny?

'What a question. You said it so solemnly. Yes, as a matter of fact, I do. Why do you ask me?'

'My father says there's a mavellously good restaurant called *L'Océan* about six or seven miles down the coast. Nothing but fish. Lobsters, soles, moules, *langoustines*, mountains of *fruits de mer*. I wondered if you'd like to go there tonight. I can have my father's car.'

For some moments she sat silent again, gently swirling the ice in her glass, as if carefully thinking the matter over.

'Thank you. Since Mrs Palgrave isn't here I think perhaps I could.'

'You mean you couldn't come if she were here?'

'Oh! no.'

'Because of the children?'

'Oh! the children will be all right. They will have dinner and afterwards play donkey. For hours.'

'Donkey?'

'It's a card game.'

Then if it wasn't the children what was it? He didn't quite get the point of it all.

'Oh! she simply doesn't approve of me – what's the word you use? – gallivanting around.'

He suddenly felt an extreme spasm of distaste for Mrs Palgrave. It was so totally unexpected that now, for once, he too was driven into silence. He even felt cut off from her presence, distracted by a queer nagging uneasiness, so that he was quite startled when Heidi said:

'Will you call for me? And what time?'

Oh! yes, he was sorry. He would call for her. Of course. What time could she be ready? Seven?

'Yes, if that is all right, at seven.'

'I've never been to this place before, but I think it should be good. My father's generally right. He's a tremendous connoisseur.'

She slowly sipped her orange juice down to the last inch or so and then looked at him for the first time with a long glance that was completely direct, easy and no longer shy.

'I'm sure,' she said, 'it will be wonderful.'

As they drove down the coast they passed wide salt flats, long artificial oblongs of drying salt glistening like virgin snow in the smouldering western sun. Out at sea a group of sardine boats, some blue, some emerald, all with sails of burning orange, were drifting westwards on an ocean of bright greengrey, every sail a tongue of flame on the vast expanse of whitewashed water.

L'Océan was white too: a sparkling low fortress set on a black bastion of rock overhanging the sea, a green flag emblazoned with a great scarlet lobster flying overhead.

'Let's get a drink outside first. My father says we must see the fish tanks. You choose your own lobster while it's still alive.'

As they sat outside on the terrace, sipping *Dubonnet*, watching the last of the sardine boats being consumed by the orange cauldron of sunset, the effect of the ocean's vastness was so great that it held him spellbound, almost embalmed. Mrs Palgrave seemed not only far away; she might never have existed.

For the first time, he noticed, Heidi was wearing a dress; a simple affair of deep blue with pipings of white at the sleeves and collar. Against it her hair looked more than usually pale blonde almost to whiteness. Her rather thin brown arms were smooth and hairless and she sat with them stretched across the table, her glass held lightly between her ringless fingers.

'What part of Germany do you come from?'

She came from Bavaria, she said. Not far from the Zugspitze, the big mountain. In winter there were great snows and she skied a lot. In summer it was beautiful for walking.

'Will you go back? I mean would you like to go back?'

That was the curious thing, she said. She really didn't want to go back. It was all very beautiful, but somehow – no, she preferred England. It gave her great satisfaction.

The very ordinariness of this conversation succeeded in deepening his own feeling of satisfaction to a point almost of serenity. He felt as if relaxing after a long, tough swim. The almost lunatic days of turbulence with Mrs Palgrave not only now seemed slightly unreal; there was an uneasy aridity about them, a brittle shadowiness from which all heat had strangely departed.

By contrast the girl sitting in front of him seemed like a bud that had only partly opened. Her physical appeal aroused in him no open excitement. He felt content merely to watch her, framed with an astonishing air of purity against sea and sunset.

'You must give me your address in London,' he said. 'We live in Berkshire, not far out. Perhaps we could meet some time.'

'Yes, I must do that. But I really don't go out very much. Because of Mrs Palgrave. I told you how it was.'

Abruptly he changed the conversation. Was she getting hungry? What did she fancy to eat? His father said the lobsters were perfect. The *sole Normande* was also marvellous, he said, and both he and his mother apparently always ate mountains and mountains of *langoustines*.

'I find them a bit messy and finicky myself. A bit tedious to unbutton, if you know what I mean.'

'I will unbutton them for you – if you would like me to.'

'Oh! would you? That's awfully nice of you. And we must drink *Montrachet*. My father says the only thing is the *Montrachet*.'

Presently they went inside the hotel to eat. Dark live lobsters crawled with slowly waving antennae about long glass tanks of green-lit water, among emerald forests of sea-weed.

'No, not for me,' Heidi said. 'The poor things look in prison, somehow. Unhappy.'

Soon they were facing prodigious pyramids of shell-fish and then a single big glass bowl of *langoustines*, flowering from rocks of ice like clusters of sea-anemones in pink and white. The *Montrachet* was cold and flinty and, as his father had predicted, excellent. He thought the *langoustines* were pretty good too, especially when, as he said more than once, you had someone to unbutton them for you. She was really spoiling him completely.

'Well, there's no harm in that, or is there?'

'Not at all, not at all. I love it.'

Outside, by now, the light had faded. Against and beyond the electric lights the sky took on the same deep bright blue as her dress and into it, at regular intervals, swept an encircling arrow of yellow, a beam from a lighthouse a mile or two away.

When the last of the *langoustines* had gone and she was thoughtfully washing her hands in a finger bowl he poured out more wine and then asked her, for the first time, if she was enjoying herself? In reply she looked down at her wet hands and said an extraordinary thing:

'More than that. For the first time since we came here I feel I am really myself.'

What did that mean? He didn't quite understand.

'With Mrs Palgrave I am never myself. She makes me afraid and I go into a shell.'

So this then, he thought, was the key to the superciliousness, the aloof cold air. But afraid? Why afraid?

'I don't know. It's just how it is.' With an abrupt smile she raised her glass to him. 'Well, cheers anyway. Your father is quite right. The wine is splendid.'

'Oh! he really knows, my father. You must meet him. He'd like you. He has such good taste.'

'Really. What flattery.'

'I know what, we'll all come here. I'll see if I can arrange it – for lunch on Sunday. If Mrs Palgrave is back she can look after the children herself for once. That'll do her no harm, will it?'

She sat very still again. He never got a single syllable in answer to that question but half way across the bay, on the drive back, he stopped the car. The beam from the lighthouse could still be seen swinging with brilliant regularity across the bay and in one of the spells of darkness it left every twenty seconds or so he kissed her lightly on the lips. Compared with the passionate bite of Mrs Palgrave's mouth it was like kissing a petal freshly unfolded.

'You're not really afraid, are you?' he said.

Perhaps the question was a stupid one but he never got an answer to it either. She lay back on the seat of the car, very still. When the beam of light flashed again her eyes were very bright and it cut across them like a sword.

Two days later he wandered along the beach, looking for her, but there was no sign of her or the children or the big yellow and white ball. Instead he caught sight of a pair of familiar golden legs and a smouldering head of auburn hair against the silver sand of the dunes.

'Hullo there, you're back.'

Mrs Palgrave was assiduously polishing her finger-nails: so assiduously that she hardly bothered to look up at him.

'When did you get in?'

'Yesterday morning.'

'Odd that I haven't seen you.'

'Odd? I had a lot of things to do. Some of them not very pleasant.'

It was now she who had the aloof, icy, supercilious air. An impulse to sit down on the sand beside her left him abruptly. He stood still, stiff and awkward.

'I haven't seen a sign of Heidi or the children either.'

'What a ghastly disappointment for you.'

A small snake of irritation curled sharply up his throat and bit the back of his mouth. She gave a long quizzical look at her nails and then made an equally long search of her handbag, finally producing a mirror.

'I think you might explain that remark.'

'Explain? I can't think why.'

She looked for fully half a minute into the mirror, without saying another word.

'I still can't think why I didn't see Heidi. She promised to meet me for coffee yesterday.'

'She could hardly meet you for coffee if she wasn't here.'

'I don't get it.'

'I've sent her home.'

The snake jabbed harshly at his throat again, making his mouth sour and sick.

'Home? You mean to Germany?'

'Of course.'

'But she'll never go. She hates the idea.'

'She's already gone. She left last night.'

He stood stiff and impotent with anger. She stared into the mirror as if he didn't exist and then suddenly he exploded in outrage.

'But good God, that's monstrous! – just like that – it's monstrous!'

'Don't shout. After all I can't have my children's maid playing fast and loose with any Tom, Dick and Harry as soon as my back's turned.'

'Fast and loose – ye gods! – all we had was a quiet, simple innocent dinner.'

At last she looked up at him, the smile on her lips cool and thin.

'Innocent? I love that word innocent. Some of your performances last week hardly belonged to the realm of innocence.'

'There was nothing like that! –'

'How disappointing for you.'

'It was not disappointing! For Christ's sake! –'

Hitherto she had treated him as a man; now she suddenly said:

'Oh! don't be a silly boy. Just go away. There's no point in getting angry.'

'Angry? I like that. It's you that's angry with me.'

She actually laughed.

'Angry? With you? Now that's really funny. On the contrary I'm very grateful.'

'I'm damned if I can think what for.'

'I've been trying to get rid of her for ages, but I never had a real good excuse. Now thanks to you I got one.'

He stood stiff and impotent with anger and humiliation. Again she stared into the mirror as if he simply didn't exist. Then suddenly she gathered up her bathing basket and handbag and stood up, her brown-green eyes absolutely stony.

'If you won't go I'm afraid I must.'

'You sound so bloody righteous somehow –'

'I don't think you quite understand. I told you what a responsibility these girls are. You simply can't have them caught up in all sorts of cheap intrigues –'

With icy contempt she turned abruptly and left him. He

stood and raged within himself with sour despair, unable to move or say a word.

The following afternoon he saw the familiar smouldering auburn head coming towards him along the promenade.

He saw at once that she was wearing a dress, a light simple affair of plain yellow, with an emerald belt, and by comparison with the brief swim-suits he had seen her wearing so often it seemed to give her a remarkably respectable, conventional air.

Walking with her was a man of sixty or so, wearing a pair of cream slacks, a navy blue blazer and a yachting cap. He carried a gold-topped walking stick and with this he sometimes pointed at objects out to sea. He too looked conventional, almost to the point of being prim.

Franklin, as Mr and Mrs Palgrave passed him, stiffened himself to say 'Good afternoon' but in the moment of passing she turned with equal stiffness and stared at the sea.

A few minutes later he was striding along the beach, out of the hot bristling sunlight into the shadow of the pines and then out into the heat of the sun again.

'Heidi,' he kept saying to himself. 'Heidi.' His echoless voice was arid with despair. The white stretch of sand in front of him was as flat and lifeless as the salt flats he had seen in the evening sun. 'Heidi – Heidi – Oh! God, Heidi, where can I find you?'

The First Day of Christmas

On the morning of Christmas Eve a thin freezing rain, with sharp needles of sleet in it, cut down on the bare bald head of Archie Burgess as he turned into a pub called *The Vine* and then went downstairs to *The Hole in the Ground*, the bar in the cellar, to order himself a milk stout and wait, hopefully, for his friend Flo Greene.

He and Flo always met in the bar at midday on Tuesdays and Fridays and in the evenings on Wednesdays and Saturdays, but although today was Friday and Christmas Eve Archie found himself in increasingly pessimistic mood about Flo. On Wednesday evening he and Flo had got themselves involved in one of those stupid, pointless tiffs that arise from nothing and then without reason grow dark and bleak. The result was that Flo had flung her way out of the bar, head high, without a word of good night.

Charitably Archie put it all down to Flo's cold or perhaps to the pressures of Christmas. Her head was completely stuffed up with cold, her nose streaming and her eyes running with moisture. With a cold like that, even at Christmastime, it was only natural for a woman to be short-tempered. Today, he told himself, he would try to make up for it all by asking Flo to marry him, but only if her cold was better. It wouldn't be right to propose to a woman, even on Christmas Eve, when she had a streaming nose and possibly a temperature.

The cellar, though dark and full of cobwebs, was snug. Fairy lights in scarlet, emerald, blue, pink and gold were hung about the ceiling. Sawdust covered the floor and bright red candles burned in black greasy bottles. The only window was covered by an iron grill at street level and through this the feet of passers-by could be seen, hurrying like lost, aimless pygmies along the pavement outside.

The only other customers in the bar were three men Archie didn't know very well: a thin whippet-faced fast-talking man in a black cap named Fred Dilbey, a pink dumpling of a man with a boiled nose nicknamed Pokey and a silent figure swathed in an old army overcoat three sizes too large for him and a thick khaki scarf wrapped so closely round his head that only a pair of grey, washed-out furtive eyes could be seen peering out of it. The three men were talking of Christmasses long ago.

Fred Dilbey did most of the talking while the others sometimes said 'Ah' or 'S'right' or merely listened. Archie sat apart, staring into the dark depths of his milk stout.

'All the bleedin' beer,' Fred Dilbey said, 'tastes the bleedin' same.'

'That does.'

'Ah.'

'I'm bleedin' tellin' you it tastes the bleedin' same. Even at Christmas time.'

'It do.'

'The same wi' the bleedin' bread. That all tastes the same. Else it don't taste o' nothink.'

'S'right. It don't taste o' nothink.'

'It's my turn,' Fred Dilbey said. 'Drink up. Two more bitters, and a whiskey, matey. After all, it's Christmas. How's your old woman, Pokey?'

Pokey stirred himself from the depths of a mild whisky coma to declare that his old woman was about like the beer. About the bleedin' same.

Coarse laughter came from Fred Dilbey, who said that's how women were. They was all as bad as one another, the old faggots.

'S'right.'

'Half the bleeders dressed like men, the other half like tarts and the rest a lot o' naggin' bitches.'

'Ah.'

'Don't you miss your old woman, Fred, then?'

Fred said he bleedin' didn't. Even at Christmas. He'd got peace now. Thirty years listening to the same nag, the same jaw, and now he'd got peace. She never could cook neither. You couldn't trust her to cook a suet dumpling, let alone a Christmas dinner, without the bleeder turned out like a bleedin' fossil.

Archie Burgess stared from his milk stout to the grill beyond the window, earnestly hoping to see the feet of Flo Greene among the passing black pygmies of Christmas shoppers. There was no doubt, in his view, that Fred Dilbey had got it all wrong. Women weren't the same, in his view, even if the beer was. Flo was very, very different. When he looked into Flo's odd, thin little face, he was transported. He felt slightly light in the head.

'I got my own Christmas dinner on now,' Fred Dilbey said. 'Anyways the Christmas pudden. Tomorrow I'll have a baked rabbit with swede turnips and mashed taters. Fit for a queen.'

From the depths of his overcoat the figure in the khaki scarf grunted and said he was damned if that didn't make him feel hungry. It sounded middlin' half-tidy, Fred's Christmas dinner did.

'You betcher bleedin' life,' Fred Dilbey said. 'It's better'n what no woman could do, I tell you that. That thick gravy, that's how I like it. She never got it thicker 'n bleedin' hog's wash.'

Archie Burgess stared at the grill. Larger blobs of sleet were falling now in the darkening midday air and he was oppressed by a cold, sinking feeling that Flo wasn't coming.

'By the way, Pokey, you bin about a few minutes. You remember a girl named Rosie Godden? Come from the marsh. Married Stony Thomas, the baker.'

Pokey said he remembered. By God, he did. For the first time he actually laughed and in such a way that his mouth seemed to water.

'Now there,' Fred Dilbey said, 'you got a woman who was a woman. Like a prize heifer. I'd like to have her in my Christmas stocking I tell you.'

You were telling him alright, Pokey said. He could see her now. Chest on her like a bushel of apples.

'They used to say it was all free, too,' Fred Dilbey said and he too started laughing. 'That mean old bastard, Stony, by God he never knowed it was going on under his bleedin' nose –'

'Got his ruddy eyes bunged up with flour,' Pokey said. The third whisky was beginning to talk a little now and he actually laughed, fruitily, for the second time. 'While he was baking at night she was –'

'You know what?' Fred Dilbey said, 'I'll tell you summat –'

'Drink up,' Pokey said. 'I'll get us all another. I'm just beginning to feel the benefit.'

In the bar the air was now so gloomy that the barman after drawing two more beers and pouring another whisky, lit two more red candles and placed them on the bar. The whole world seemed suddenly much brighter.

'Lead kindly light,' Fred Dilbey said, 'What was I saying?'

'How the bleedin' hell should we know? You never said it.'

This time Pokey and Fred actually laughed together, in coughing alcoholic chorus, while Archie Burgess took slow cold sips from his milk stout and stared at dark feet passing in the falling snow. Every moment there seemed, he thought, to be more and more snow and fewer and fewer feet.

'It was about these sovereigns,' Fred Dilbey said. 'Ten gallon of 'em. Gold.'

'Ten gallon? How much is ten gallon? I mean what was they worth?'

'I mean they was all in gallon measures. Like you put apples in. She found 'em in an old flour trough in the bakehouse after he was dead. All locked up.'

'Saved 'em all up for Christmas every year, I'll bet.'

Archie stared into his diminishing milk stout, wondering if to order another, and thought with increasing melancholy of Flo. Flo wasn't pretty: he knew that. Nor was she exactly young any more. Nor was there much flesh on her. In fact you could even call her skinny. But whenever he saw her thin sallow face coming along the street or into the bar he was unbearably touched by the small bright black eyes and the thin fragile lips that curved exactly like the petals of a rose.

'With a woman like that and a pint o' beer that tasted like beer and a piece o' bread that tasted like bread,' Fred Dilbey said, 'you could have a Christmas that was a Christmas. What more could you want?'

'Only a few golden sovereigns,' Pokey said and laughed again.

While Fred and Pokey guffawed into their glasses Archie got up, went to the bar and ordered himself another milk stout. It was on the tip of his tongue to ask the barman if he'd seen anything of Flo that morning but he finally decided against it and the barman, looking out at the increasingly larger flakes of snow, said he thought it was settling in for a real white Christmas. Archie said he thought so too and took his milk stout and went back to sit on his chosen barrel.

'Ten gallon. That's a hell of a lot of sovereigns,' Pokey said. 'She was what you might call a good catch.'

'She had some made into earrings,' Fred Dilbey said. 'A pair on each side.'

Archie was not only unbearably moved by the sight of Flo. He longed desperately that she should replace a wife that had been able to cook a good hot beef stew, bake a carraway cake, and even make almond toffee at week-ends. He even dared to think, with something like passion, of one day kissing Flo and perhaps, eventually, of sharing a bed with her. His heart was filled with a small slow ache when he thought of it all.

'I can see her now,' Fred Dilbey said, 'of a summer evening, sitting outside *The Green Man* at Market Broughton. Chest like a bushel o' ripe apples, like you said, and the sovereigns bobbin' up and down in her ears like gold cherries. God, I tell you – drink up, Pokey, I'll buy you another bleedin' whisky. Damn it, it's Christmas!'

Laughing again, Fred Dilbey got up to order more of the beer that didn't taste of anything and two more whiskies. You'd got to keep the weather out somehow, he said to the barman and with a trembling hand poured one of the whiskies into his beer.

'She'd got a laugh on her like a bell,' he said. The beer and the whisky had begun to talk together now. An aura positively rosy, as if from the light of a good fire, hung about the cellar. 'You could have heard her in the next parish.'

Archie stared from the milk stout to the diminishing numbers of passing feet. In the short intervals between the voices of Fred and Pokey he could fairly hear the deadly silence of the darkening Christmas Eve. Flo, he told himself, would never turn out in this weather. It would be crazy with her cold.

'I saw her once in a purple dress,' Fred Dilbey said, 'and with three sovereigns in each ear. She looked like the bleedin' Bank of England.'

Archie was moved by this last sentence to think again of Flo. Her ears, far from looking like the Bank of England, were very small. They seemed to be no bigger, he often thought, than snails. They were extraordinarily white and might have been made of china. You saw them best when she took her hat off. Suddenly it was almost as if she might have been undressing. The small unexpectedly naked ears gave him the same inexpressible sensation.

Loudly Fred Dilbey proclaimed that Rosie Godden was a woman in a million. They didn't come like her any more, with chests like that and golden sovereigns in their ears. Nowadays, like the bleedin' beer, they all tasted the same.

'How often do you have a taste?' Pokey said.

'I'd rather,' Fred said, 'have a good rabbit dinner.'

Suddenly Archie wondered if he shouldn't buy a quarter bottle of whisky and take it round, as a sort of Christmas peace-offering, to Flo. It would do her cold good if she took it with hot lemon. Or perhaps port would be better. For some five minutes he debated with himself on this and then regretfully decided against it. She might think he was trying to bribe her back, sort of.

'Well, it's gone one o'clock,' Fred Dilbey said. 'I got to see how my Christmas pudden's cooking –'

'Is she still alive?' Pokey said.

'Oh! dead,' Fred Dilbey said. 'Dead.'

The word fell on Archie's ears like a sepulchral knell. At the same moment a pair of feet, a woman's, in small black shoes, paused beyond the grill, on the pavement outside. Briefly Archie stared at them, saw them as belonging to Flo and then watched them move out of sight.

It was suddenly as if by some miracle Flo had turned up after all and as suddenly and completely moved out of his life. He found himself struggling with the unbearable conviction that she was out there on the pavement, in the snow, vanishing for ever. The ache produced by this became abruptly so large that it expanded into pain. He picked up his milk stout to finish it off, suddenly felt sick and set it down again.

'Well, I bid you all good morning,' Fred Dilbey said, voice husky, narrow legs as unsteady as a foal's as he rose to depart. 'All good morning.'

'Morning, Fred,' Pokey said. 'Don't do nothing we wouldn't do.'

'Some folks talk a lot.' Fred Dilbey looked with a lugubrious watery eye at Archie Burgess, staring down at his milk stout. 'I said all good morning. All.'

Archie, neither listening nor speaking, found himself suddenly gripped by the conviction that if he didn't move quickly it would be too late. Flo would be gone for keeps.

He started to hurry from the bar, up the stairs and into the street, leaving his milk stout unfinished on its barrel in the candlelight.

Then as he reached the top of the stairs he changed his mind again, half ran back to the bar and said to the barman:

'Give me half a bottle of port. How much? No, better make it a bottle.'

His hands were trembling as he picked up the bottle and went back up the stairs. Out in the street snow was slicing the dark air with thick fast flakes. There was no sign of Flo. Nor was there any sign, anywhere, of women with golden sovereigns in their ears.

The Black Magnolia

HARTLEY Wilkinson Spencer was a bachelor of nearly fifty. If he had been a stick of rock the word 'Good' would have been printed clean down the entire centre of him.

He was in fact not at all unlike a stick of rock : face brightest pink, body slim and erect, prematurely white hair thick, handsome, strongly curled, his general air wholesome, saintly, virtuous to a point of sugariness, splendidly pure.

On Sunday morning he read lessons in Chapel; on Sunday afternoons he delivered homilies both stern and brotherly to Bible Classes; on frequent week nights he read papers to various gatherings on such illuminating subjects as *The Place of God in the Welfare State, Prison Reform* and *To Hang or Not to Hang?* By day he worked with an acumen not far short of cunning at the book-binding business left him by his father. Everywhere, continually, he toiled massively for charities, rallies, good causes. With almost patriarchal dedication he presided on committees of every possible kind. He was a magistrate and a Justice of the Peace. And since the Ten Commandments were not quite ample enough to satisfy his pious appetite he had invented several more, including 'after all, business is business', 'thou shalt not cheat or at least be observed to be cheating' and 'the greatest good for the greatest number – the number being Number One'.

Two or three days a week he went to London by train : not always the same train, but sometimes as early as eight-thirty in the morning, sometimes as late as four o'clock in the afternoon. Always the clean, upright figure with the handsome white hair had a look of saintliness, almost that of a prophet, incredibly pure and strong as it stood out above the weaker mortal flesh of the rest of the world.

Late one April he found himself the victim of three extraordinary coincidences. On the London train he saw the same woman, age about forty-five, at three different times of day: once on a train at nine-thirty in the morning, then at midday, and the third time at four o'clock in the afternoon.

On two of these occasions she was wearing the same attire and it was perhaps because her complete outfit was in the shade of the most brilliant acid green, a colour so many people regarded as unlucky, that his attention was first drawn to her. Over her bright green dress she wore a coat of the same colour trimmed at the collar and cuffs with light black fur; her small round hat, which she wore pushed well back from her face, was also of black fur; her gloves and shoes too were black; round her neck she wore a necklace of rather large beads of an even brighter green than her coat and dress, with earrings to match in the shape of a star.

On the first two occasions he merely saw her on the station platform, waiting for the train. On the third occasion he had a sudden conviction that she deliberately got into the same carriage with him, though at the time he couldn't think why. Another striking thing about her that afternoon was that she was carrying a large bouquet of flowers, among them narcissi, tulips, sprays of red flowering currant, pink and white camellias and a few branches of pure mooncream magnolia.

After she had laid the bouquet on the seat beside her she put on a pair of tinted horn-rimmed glasses and started to read a book: or rather, as he presently discovered, merely to look at it. For twenty or thirty seconds she would stare at a page and then rapidly flick over another dozen or more pages and then stare at another.

All this went on for a quarter of an hour or so before she suddenly took off the glasses, laid them with the book on the seat, leaned forward and said:

'It is Mr Hartley Spencer isn't it?'

'Yes.'

'I hope you'll forgive my introducing myself.' She suddenly smiled with a look of deliberate enchantment, her large brown eyes restless and bright. 'I'm Vanessa La Farge. I've just taken over Waterfield Court. You probably know it?'

'Of course. But oddly enough I've never been there. It always looks immensely attractive from the road.'

'The reason I spoke to you is because I'm told you're the great one for charities. Raising funds and things.'

'Well, one tries one's best.'

'I think that's over-modest. I heard you raised a thousand and something for the Turkish earthquake thing.'

'I fancy it was nearly fifteen hundred by the time we'd finished. I forget the final figure.'

She made an expansive gesture with her left hand, saying it was marvellous anyway. Her wedding ring flashed and for some reason it eased the slight tension he had experienced ever since she had joined him in the carriage. To be alone with a woman invariably made him taut and defensive and moreover there were undoubted dangers to be associated with travelling alone with a strange woman on a train. You never knew.

'It's rather warm in here, don't you think?' she suddenly said and got up and slipped off her coat, at the same time slightly pushing back the neck of her dress. This gesture served not only to bring back his feeling of tension but to make it rather worse. 'Not that one should complain after the wretched April we've had.'

'I know. Rain almost every day.'

'What I was going to ask you was this – do you think I might talk you into helping me with a big charity thing on June the first? Well, not exactly charity – it's for the Florence Art disaster thing.'

'June the first?' Hartley Spencer, with prompt efficiency, took out his pocket diary and looked up the date. 'I'm awfully sorry, but I've an important business lunch in Nottingham that day.'

'Then let's make it the second. I know a man like you must be absolutely inundated with requests and all that.'

'Yes, the second, I could do the second.'

'How marvellously nice of you. I think we should do something for art for a change, don't you? It shouldn't always be for people. Do you know Florence?'

No, Hartley Spencer said, he didn't know Florence. Nor, though he refrained from saying so, did he quite agree with her about art and people. Pictures and that sort of thing were not much in his line.

'I lived for a time in Florence,' she said. 'Well, rather just outside it. I got to know the Tuscan countryside. It's very real to me.'

As the train slightly changed its course the afternoon sunlight poured with increased warmth and brilliance into the carriage, suddenly drawing out the honey breath of tulips and the sharper fragrance of narcissi.

'The spring there was lovely. Not like ours of course, but warmer, beautiful –'

'What exactly, if I may ask, did you want me to do?'

'Well, I'm open to any suggestions. One thing I'm going to do is to charge five shillings as an entrance fee and for that you get free sherry. Not just a measly glass, but a good whack. I find people don't start spending until you've got them steamed up a bit.'

'H'm.'

With this half-stifled syllable Hartley Spencer withheld his opinion on the powers of sherry to induce heavier spending. In his work for charities he had found no need for alcohol.

'There'll be a plant and flower stall. Would you care to run that?'

Hartley Spencer confessed that he wasn't a great one on flowers. It wasn't that they left him cold exactly – he just didn't know half of them from another. A little bemused, he looked at her bouquet. For instance he hardly knew if the pink branches were apple-blossom or not. He knew the tulips of course, but he hadn't the remotest idea what the big creamy-white thing was.

'Oh! surely you know magnolia.'

'I have to plead ignorance I'm afraid.'

Hartley Spencer said this not in fact as if he were ignorant but as if the pretence of ignorance made him superior.

'They're in their full glory now, the magnolias,' she said. 'They must have been planted twenty-five or thirty years ago and they've got to be really big trees, most of them. Especially the black one.'

'I beg your pardon? The what one?'

'The black one.'

Hartley Spencer smiled with saint-like indulgence.

'Really? I don't think I've ever heard of a black flower.'

'Well, you've heard of one now.'

'Once when I was a boy my father took me to a friend's garden and showed me a green rose but I always had a sneaking impression that it was dyed. Is yours dyed?'

Vanessa La Farge suddenly felt herself sharply annoyed by this remark.

'I'm sorry you doubt my word.'

'Oh! I don't exactly doubt your word. But you must admit it does sound a bit like a fairy tale.'

'I'm not in the habit of telling fairy tales.'

For a minute or more the air in the carriage grew icy. Mrs La Farge put on her tinted spectacles and in silence stared at her book.

At last Hartley Spencer, now smiling in a way that was on the verge of being supercilious, said:

'Perhaps you look at it through your dark spectacles.'

Mrs La Farge, now keeping her temper with difficulty, answered this by saying:

'It's name is *Soulangeana nigra* and *nigra*, in my dictionary, means black.'

'I suppose it does. I was never very good at Latin.'

After this remark, which she didn't bother to answer, a great cold gap opened up between them. For a prolonged silent period, during which the outer suburbs of South London began to show up beyond the carriage windows, Mrs La Farge simply looked at her book with a blank, restrained stare.

Soon, as the train began to run into the inner suburbs, Hartley Spencer felt the need to break the ice of the long, embarrassing silence and at last said:

'We didn't finish talking about your charity affair.'

'Oh? I thought we did.'

'Well, anyway, what can I do to help?'

'Nothing, thank you.'

The only other words they exchanged that afternoon were a flat 'Good day' from her, which he answered with an excessively stiff 'Good-bye'.

With the large bouquet of flowers lying across one arm Mrs La Farge finally floated caustically, rather than walked, from the train.

Following her down the platform, Hartley Spencer suddenly found himself staring at her disappearing legs. As he did so a curious guilty spasm shot through him and suddenly even he, inexperienced as he was in the shape of the female body, was startled into a realization that they were very beautiful.

A moment later he swiftly averted his eyes and turned his thoughts to more important things.

The meeting with Vanessa La Farge on the train had on Hartley Spencer much of the effect often experienced by boys when kissed, for the first time, by a girl at a party or in a meadow on the way home from school. As adolescence is rapturously, painfully shattered by such experiences Hartley Spencer was mentally disrupted in middle age.

It was typical of him that he suffered this unexpected turmoil with a nagging conscience that imposed a degree of pain. For some days he found himself afflicted with a mental need to make amends for all he had said in the railway carriage. From his deep well of inherent goodness rose a positive hunger to apologize.

At first he felt he should do this by means of a letter. Then he considered, and rejected, the idea of the telephone. Neither, though clearly less painful than meeting Vanessa La Farge face to face, would really satisfy the demands of a conscience so wholesome and strong. He realized, eventually, that there was nothing for it but to meet her, express his infinite regret and hope to be forgiven. It was altogether not unlike a schoolboy going to a headmaster to confess some grave misdeed.

On a warm evening in early May Hartley Spencer parked his car in a gateway a quarter of a mile from Mrs La Farge's rather large Georgian house set in a park-like landscape illuminated with many enormous flowering chestnuts, both pink and white, along the banks of a stream. It seemed to him that a walk for the rest of the way to the house was the best and only possible means of calming his embarrassed, even tortured thoughts.

When he at last arrived in the garden it was to find a further series of embarrassments awaiting him. He was first of all caught completely unawares by meeting Vanessa La Farge face to face on the terrace of the house, where she was sitting with a friend. The uncomfortable fact of finding her not alone was further complicated by the fact that the friend was another woman, quite as strikingly attractive as Mrs La Farge herself but at least ten years younger. The entire purpose of his visit now seemed to lie shattered at his feet and he realized with further acute pain that he could no longer apologize. He stood on the terrace hopelessly flustered and frustrated.

By contrast Vanessa La Farge was cool, friendly and serene. The incident of the railway carriage might never have happened.

'What a nice surprise, Mr Spencer.'

'I was just passing – I hope it isn't too awkward a moment –'

'Absolutely not. In fact we were just talking about you. May I introduce Miss O'Connor? Kitty O'Connor – Mr Hartley Spencer.'

Hartley Spencer now found himself gazing into a pair of dark eyes that had on them a bloom like that of grapes. Their returning liquid, misty stare had not only a certain mysterious quality that was also mischievously impish but succeeded in creating yet another embarrassment even more acute than Mrs Vanessa

La Farge's remark that the two women had been talking about him. He had no idea what to say except 'Good evening', at the same time ruffling a flustered hand through his hair.

'Kitty's Irish. From Limerick. She's helping me with the charity thing. But you know what the Irish are. Quite impractical. You can never pin them down.'

Kitty O'Connor laughed at this with bell-like glee, her voice fresh as a mountain stream.

'You'll stay for a drink?' Vanessa La Farge said. 'Sit down while I go and organize something. Talk to Kitty.'

Vanessa La Farge went into the house. Hartley Spencer sat down in the bamboo garden chair she had left and looked obligingly for some twenty seconds or so at Kitty O'Connor, who was wearing a striking pink linen dress in colour not unlike that of the pink chestnuts. Now and then she caught his uneasy eyes with an impish flash of her own, as if trying to tease him into opening the conversation.

At last he said :

'Were you really talking about me? I'm afraid you couldn't have given me a good report if you were. I fear I'm in bad books.'

'Oh? I didn't get that impression at all.'

Kitty O'Connor's dreamy Irish accent, liquid as her eyes, seemed to hang on the warm May air.

'I'm afraid I doubted her word about a tree she has in the garden. A black magnolia.'

'She was telling me that.'

'I looked it up in a book on shrubs. Of course it is *nigra*. Meaning black.'

'It's more a purple shade. A dark sort of plum. I think she calls it black just to tease people. She's the great teaser sometimes.'

Kitty O'Connor laughed again, her voice beautifully gay and clear, and Hartley Spencer half got the impression that she might almost have been laughing at him. He was unused to gaiety.

'I never take her too seriously,' Kitty O'Connor said. 'There's a little of the Irish in her too.'

A still slightly embarrassed Hartley Spencer suddenly said that the garden was very beautiful.

'She does a lot of it herself. It keeps her occupied now that Edward's away.'

Hartley Spencer presumed she meant Mr La Farge?

'International lawyer, shipping mostly. Goes away on big tricky lawsuits for ages and ages, in the name o' God.'

Hartley Spencer, unused to hearing the name of God taken in vain, sat further embarrassed and was intensely glad to see Vanessa La Farge, a moment later, appearing with a tray of drinks and glasses. It relieved him to get up and rush to help her dutifully with the tray.

'Now, what shall it be? Gin, whisky, sherry or what? Kitty?'

'A load of gin with a touch of French, dear. I've a craving thirst.'

'Ice?'

'Lots of ice. A glacier of ice.'

Ice tinkled into Kitty O'Connor's glass with a sound not unlike the echo of her high laughter.

'And you, Mr Spencer?'

'Oh! nothing for me, thank you, not for me.'

'Nothing!'

'Well, just plain bitter lemon if you have plain bitter lemon.'

'Damn, I didn't bring it.'

'I'll go,' Kitty O'Connor said. 'I need some cigarettes anyway. Just bitter lemon? Is that all?'

Just plain bitter lemon, Hartley Spencer said, still further embarrassed to be a bother.

Alone with him, Vanessa La Farge poured herself a handsome gin-and-tonic and remarked, coolly, that it was nice of him to have dropped in, surprised though she was to see him.

'I felt I had to say that I was sorry for what I said on the train.'

'Oh! nonsense. I never gave it another thought.'

'Really? Still, I am sorry.'

'Oh! life's too short for these things.'

'Is the magnolia still in bloom? Miss O'Connor says it's more purple than black.'

'It's still out. We'll go and see it when we've had a drink or two. I've been gardening all afternoon. We're making a new water garden. I need a stiffener or two. Don't you ever?'

'Never.'

On Kitty O'Connor's return with the bitter lemon she and Vannessa La Farge had a number of generous stiffeners, at the same time contributing a good deal of laughter to the evening air.

Now and then they also discussed the charity affair.

'What we need is some good, original ideas,' Vanessa La Farge said. 'What about it, Mr Spencer?'

Hartley Spencer suggested he organize a raffle or perhaps guessing the weight of a sack of apples. He had once done that with great success. Peals of laughter greeted these exciting suggestions and Vanessa La Farge said:

'What about Kitty giving kisses at a guinea a time? That's an idea.'

'Two guineas for a bang on the lips. I'm game.'

Hartley Spencer's attempt to join in the laughter that greeted this left him with a mere wry smile.

'All right, kisses it is then, in the name o' God,' Kitty O'Connor said. Her merriment, inspired by further glaciers of gin, was increasing every moment. 'Shall I be putting you down for five guineas' worth, Mr Spencer?'

Hartley Spencer could only receive the offer with a second thin wry smile.

'No, no, I'm serious about this. The Forbes-Walters had a film star down to do it at their garden party a couple of years ago and they cooked up a hundred and fifty quid. They even had a character who offered fifty quid for more interesting privileges.'

'My God,' Kitty O'Connor said. 'Spare me.'

'Many a girl,' Vanessa La Farge said, 'would do it voluntarily and for nothing.'

Hartley Spencer could only sip in silence at his bitter lemon.

At last Vanessa La Farge said it was time to walk down to see the black magnolia before darkness fell and, if Mr Spencer would like it, the new water garden. She was really rather pleased with the way the new water garden was shaping up.

'Coming, Kitty?'

'I've seen it. You two go.'

An intoxicating scent of lilacs filled the air down the path to the water garden. Completely lost on Hartley Spencer it nevertheless woke in Vanessa La Farge expressions of rapture almost sensuous.

'It always reminds me of Vienna and Mozart and Schubert and all that. The scent starts making the most marvellous pictures for me.'

This too was lost on Hartley Spencer, who said:

'Pictures? I don't understand.'

'I suppose,' she said, 'it's a sort of teleprinter thing in the brain. The brain photographs the scent and records it as a picture. Years after, ages after, there comes a moment when you smell the same perfume again and the brain responds with the picture.'

Hartley Spencer walked unresponsively past a huge white lilac, its heavy double trusses of flower like milky drooping breasts. She might have been talking Greek to him.

'Haven't you ever had that experience? Doesn't it ever strike you as a miraculous thing?'

In a flat voice Hartley Spencer confessed he had never had that experience.

'Perhaps I'm hypersensitive in these matters,' she said. 'Violets do terrific things to me. And honeysuckle. Honeysuckle's a positive torture.'

Hartley Spencer, to whom it had never even remotely occurred that flowers and their fragrance had the power to affect emotions, let alone to torture, was trying to frame some answer to all this when she said :

'You'll never guess what does things to Kitty. We were talking about it the other day.'

'I suppose the peat bogs of Ireland or something.'

'Grass. Not hay. But grass – just grass bruised by people walking on it. You know that juicy aroma? She says it sends her wild.'

Like a man thrown suddenly with neither direction nor compass into a territory utterly strange and unexplored Hartley Spencer walked on in a silent daze, until at last aroused by her simple statement :

'Well, there it is.'

She halted before the black magnolia. Its petals, in the lowering evening sun, had the same dark bloom, pink-black, seen sometimes on Indian skins.

'I know it isn't truly black,' she said. 'But there it is.'

Some instinct prompted Hartley Spencer to bend forward, take one of the dark magnolia flowers in his hand and hold it to his face. The heavy chalice of petals was quite without perfume.

'Oh! there's no scent. And actually this dark one isn't a favourite of mine. I much prefer the pure white one.'

'Once again,' Hartley Spencer said, releasing the big magnolia flower, 'I do apologize.'

'Oh! do stop apologizing, Mr Spencer.'

'I'm sorry. But things like that always make me uneasy.'

'I've already told you – life's too short for these things.'

They walked on to the water garden. Pausing now and then, she explained her intentions. Already part of the stream had been damned, creating a series of waterfalls. The sound of water spilling over shallow walls of rock fell like light music on the summer air. There were also to be a series of tributaries in turn passing into pools, in turn to be filled with water lilies, water arums and water grasses.

Sometimes as she explained all this she stood framed against the lowering sun, arms upstretched in such a way that the taut curve of her breast and the smooth spoon of her back were silhouettes of olive green. The breathless air by the stream had in it a quality of suspense that was magical. The sound of falling water was a rain of silver scales.

In such an atmosphere another man might have been driven, even a little tortured, to express an excited delight in being alone in the presence of a woman of singular attraction. Hartley Spencer merely said, with solemnity:

'And will you have fish?'

God. I must tell Kitty this, she thought.

'They tell me you have to put in molluscs, fresh water mussels, to oxygenate the water. Do you?'

'I'm sure you do.'

As they began to walk back a nightingale began singing high up in a row of silver poplars beyond the stream, but the entrancement of this, as with the lilacs, her own attraction and the music of falling water, was also utterly lost on him. Nor did he even remotely sense that she was teasing him with the coolest deliberation when she said:

'And what did you think of Kitty's idea of selling kisses at a price?'

'Did she mean in public?'

'Oh! gracious, no. We'd have a tent or something. There has to be a little mystery.'

'I I'm. Do you approve?'

'Certainly. I'd sell a few guineas' worth myself. After all what's better than being kissed in a good cause?'

For some long time after Hartley Spencer had left the two women sat on the terrace of the house, drinking glasses of cool white Alsatian wine. Now and then Kitty O'Connor's mischievous laughter floated, very like scales of rippling water, into the darkening summer air.

'Nobody,' she said once, 'can be that good. No one man can have that amount of goodness in him. It isn't human. Even virgins have some vices.'

'I've a deep suspicion that virginity is more painful in the male.'

'Really? And would you care to try to remove it?'

'Well, God knows he's handsome enough. You can't deny he's handsome. You try. I fancy it might be like eating raw fish.'

'Please.'

After this exchange they again laughed a good deal, until at last Vanessa La Farge, pouring the last of the white wine, said: 'What about a little more of this? Another bottle? Good idea?'

'Heavenly idea. After all we've got to comfort our poor starved female souls with something.' Again Kitty O'Connor suddenly laughed with impish delight. 'No, what he clearly needs are the attentions of a wanton woman.'

'Are you, by any chance, looking at me?'

'Not necessarily.' Once again Kitty O'Connor lifted the music of her voice high into the dark summer air. 'I was once not unwanton myself.'

The thin grey alpaca suit that Hartley Spencer was wearing on the following Thursday evening gave him a slightly clerical air. The day had been one of windless serenity.

A maid at Waterfield Court told him that Mrs La Farge was down at the swimming pool. He took this to mean that the pool was somewhere by the water gardens but the maid said 'Oh! no sir, it's the other way. On the west side of the house,' and at the same time gave his handsome face a covetous sideways glance of her dark young eyes that quite unnerved him.

He was still recovering from this when he found Vanessa La Farge by the pool, a circular one painted thrush egg blue, with a pleasant colonnaded bath-house at one end. Mrs La Farge was alone and if the covetous, slightly saucy glance of her maid had unnerved him the sight of a naked body whose only covering consisted of three modest black triangles actually brought a flush to his cheeks and a sudden prickle of cold sweat to the nape of his neck.

She was lying on her back in front of the bath-house, in full sun, on a white foam rubber bed. Her skin was the colour of honey. Her navel might have been a soft dark bee. Undressed, she looked younger than he had always supposed her to be and in a confused effort not to look at the more intimate parts of her body he hastily turned his attention to her feet. The toe nails, to his even greater confusion, were painted a singular orange carmine.

'Oh! how nice to see you, Mr Spencer. Did you bring your swim trunks? Kitty isn't here I'm afraid. She's gone into town to get the evening papers. Still, all the luckier for me.'

'I'm afraid I didn't know you had a pool.'

'Oh! we can lend you trunks. I'll telephone up to the house. The maid will bring them down.'

'Oh! no, no, please. I really mustn't stay that long.'

'But you must stay for Kitty. She'll be desperately disappointed if she misses you.'

During this conversation she sat up. Her altered position now caused the upper triangles of her costume to slip a little, revealing the outer and upper edges of a pair of fine taut breasts. His acute embarrassment at this became acuter still as she suddenly lifted both arms to her hair, smoothing it down with both hands and at the same time revealing the dark shadows of her armpits.

'Wouldn't you like a drink? There's everything in the bath-house. We always run a bar down here. Do help yourself. And if you'd like to be a darling pour me a gin-and-tonic. A nice large one, with plenty of ice.'

She too gave him a winning smile beside which the covetous smile of the maid seemed quite innocuous, so much so that as he poured out drinks in the bath-house he found himself actually trembling.

'Thanks. You're a darling.' She took her drink from him, curled her legs gracefully and sat on them, looking him full in the face. 'Haven't you got one yourself?'

'No, thanks. I had rather a late tea.'

'Well, cheers anyway. Perhaps you'll have one when Kitty comes.'

There seemed to be nothing he could say to this and for fully another half minute he sat silent, trying desperately to avoid the trap of eyes, breasts, navel, painted toe nails and the provocative curve of her thighs.

'Oh! speaking of Kitty – don't let on that I said so, but you've made quite a conquest there.'

He sat on the edge of the pool completely dumbfounded, able to mutter no more than 'I – I really – a what?' at the same time slightly blushing.

'Oh! don't underestimate yourself. Don't be modest, Mr Spencer.'

'I'm afraid you must have misinterpreted –'

'Not on your life. What do you think my eyes are for?'

'I hardly know what to – I wouldn't want to give Miss O'Connor any wrong impression.'

Vanessa La Farge immediately gave a deliberately provocative laugh that filled him with vastly increased discomfort and then said:

'Don't you think she's marvellously pretty?'

'Oh! I suppose she is attractive.'

'Suppose! She's a beauty. You wait till you see her in a swim suit.'

The brief and sensational nature of one swim suit having reduced him to a state of near nervous panic Hartley Spencer found himself secretly and inwardly running from the experience of another with something like the terror of a man being pursued by a hostile dog.

'Won't you really have a swim? I'm sure Kitty will when she comes. The pool's heated, by the way. We've been swimming quite late at night. Great fun. In the dark one feels quite – well, you know, uninhibited.'

He could only guess at what this meant and at the same time profoundly hope it wasn't true.

'Anyway, what new ideas have you come up with for the fête? I'll bet you've had some splendid ones.'

Hartley Spencer gave a difficult sort of cough and now found himself facing yet another moment of acute embarrassment.

'Well, actually that's what I came to talk about. I'm afraid I shan't be available to help after all.'

'Oh! Mr Spencer, you can't do that to us!'

'I'm most awfully sorry, but I now find I have to be in Manchester and Salford on that day and for the following two days. I really do apologize '

'Mr Spencer, Mr Spencer. How could you?'

Hartley Spencer sat in misery, conscience-stricken, incapable of saying a word.

'We were absolutely relying on you. You've got such a reputation for these things.'

'I know how – of course I'll give you a subscription – I – would five guineas? –'

'Oh! no you don't. No buying yourself out and taking a discount on Kitty's kisses. Oh! no.'

'Please, Mrs La Farge. Don't make it any worse for me.' Vanessa La Farge now sat up, body at first straight, knees together, eyes transfixing him liquidly and completely. Then she moved the upper part of her body forward, so that once again her fine expanded breasts seemed about to escape from their black triangular covering.

'I believe you're trying to back out deliberately.'

Hartley Spencer, who was in fact desperately trying to do exactly this, stuttered that he was honestly doing no such thing, no such thing.

'On your honour?'

'On my honour,' Hartley Spencer said, thus committing himself to an unprecedented, downright lie.

'I don't know whether to believe you or not.'

Agonized, he repeated that it was true, on his word of honour, word of honour.

In answer she leaned forward a little further and then suddenly, as if prompted by a sudden rush of modesty, gave the triangles that barely covered her breasts a slight hitch that merely had the effect of making them seem rounder, tauter and more conspicuous.

'Well, I can tell you one thing, honour or not. You'll be out of Kitty's good books from now on. She won't love you any more.'

The word love fell on him like a pain. More painful still, she drew attention to herself yet again by smoothing her hands up and down her honey-coloured thighs, causing him to say desperately:

'I really think I must go now, Mrs La Farge. I'm really awfully sorry about – of course I'll send you the cheque.'

'Oh! no you don't. Here comes Kitty.'

He turned to see Kitty O'Connor coming from the direction of the house dressed in a summer frock of geranium red, the taut sleeveless simplicity of which gave the impression that it was the only garment she was wearing.

He rose to greet her, only to hear Vanessa La Farge cause him further pain by saying:

'Just in time, Kitty. He was on the verge of leaving. If you can believe such a thing.'

'Bad man,' Kitty said. 'How could you, Mr Spencer?'

The slight pout she gave him was more provocative than any smile and he could find no word of answer. Vanessa La Farge found it instead and, laughing, said:

'Entertain Kitty while I go and get dressed. I find it a little cool. That's unless Kitty wants to swim?'

'No, I'm quite happy talking to Mr Spencer.'

The mischievous simplicity of this remark wrapped him into a further tangle of confusion, out of which he temporarily extricated himself by hastily obeying Vanessa La Farge's smoothly imperative order:

'Get Kitty a drink. I'm sure she'd love one. Be a dear and be a barman.'

Hartley Spencer retired to the colonnaded bath-house shelter to be barman, preceded by the honey figure of Vanessa La Farge. There, while he mixed a long iced gin-and-French for Kitty O'Connor he was vastly disturbed by the voice of Vanessa La Farge calling from one of the dressing cubicles:

'Mix me one too, will you? Lying in the sun always makes me thirsty.'

About half a minute later a naked honey-coloured arm reached out from the half-open cubicle door and her voice said:

'Hand it to me will you, dear? I'm not quite ready to come out yet.'

As he prepared to hand over the gin-and-tonic Hartley Spencer found it impossible to resist the sensational impression that he was a mere few inches away from a completely naked female body. Her low 'Thank you, darling' seemed husky. Nor, for once in his life, could he escape the strong but indefinable scent of some anointing powder, oil or perfume that floated from the cubicle and he instantly recalled her remark on the insidious sensory effects of fragrances.

'Don't neglect Kitty, will you? I know she's been dying to talk to you.'

He escaped to the pool with slight relief, only to find that Kitty O'Connor had moved herself to a stone garden seat, on which she was now sitting with knees drawn up, graceful stockingless legs fully revealed.

'Not drinking?' she said.

He confessed again that he'd had rather a late tea. A slight spasm or two of indigestion had in fact put him in occasional discomfort and he quickly suppressed a short low belch.

'Cheers. And what marvellous ideas have you been cooking up for Vanessa?'

Miserably he had once again to confess his regretful inability to help at the fête. She at once uttered a blasphemous 'Holy Mary, that won't do at all. She'll be broken-hearted. You might just as well clip the wings of an angel.'

The Irish exaggerations, delivered with a silken drawl, added further to the discomforts already brought about by naked limbs, insidious perfumes, indigestion and the fact of being repeatedly hailed as darling.

'I'm most awfully sorry, but it simply can't be helped. I simply must go to Manchester. It's something I simply can't get out of. Of course I've promised Mrs La Farge a cheque.'

'And a mighty fat one, I hope.' She patted the stone seat with the palm of her hand. 'Anyway come and sit by me. Let's be having a tête-à-tête before Vanessa comes.'

Wretchedly he sat on the seat, resigning himself to the uncomfortable prospect of the tête-à-tête. Gin-and-French in hand, Kitty O'Connor made no move to change her attitude on the seat and with legs still provocatively upraised begged him in a silky voice, and in the name o' God :

'Does this mean I'm going to be deprived of the privilege and pleasure of selling my wares to you?'

He could only take a long painful breath, with nothing to say.

'You disappoint me terribly,' she said. 'I was looking forward to that. I thought you'd be my first customer.'

She started to wet her lips with her tongue. They immediately shone with the heightened geranium red of her dress. Then she looked dubiously, with a slight pout, into her glass and said :

'You didn't put more than a pint o' gin in this, did you? Would you mind? I can't feel a thing.'

Aware of having failed in a duty he went back to the bath-house, there to find Vanessa La Farge, bare-footed, wrapped in a yellow bath-towel, in the act of renewing her own gin-and-tonic, a feat made precarious by the fact that she had only one hand to pour the drink and one to hold up the bath-towel.

'I'm afraid I'm not much of a barman,' he said. 'I was a little miserly with the gin.'

'Oh! splosh it in. She likes it the full strength, our Kitty. Splosh it in.'

Dutifully he sploshed it in.

'And be nice to her. You know what I said. About that conquest. I'll be twenty minutes or more yet. I've got a couple of telephone calls to make –'

He returned to Kitty, who took the newly fortified drink, sniffed at it, laughed impishly, said that was more like the real McCoy and that he was the beautiful man.

Again the Irish exaggerations flowed silkily, leaving him mute. Her eyes smiled at him liquidly while his own again found no place in which to rest with any sort of ease.

'Gin,' she suddenly said after another deep drink or two, 'always makes me amorous.'

Hartley Spencer, who had never drunk gin in his life and hadn't ever thought of its amorous properties either, could only stare at the blue still water of the pool.

'Well,' she said at last, 'and how many guineas' worth can I sell you?'

'I don't think we need make any sort of transaction. I'll gladly give just the cheque –'

'Here, that's not very flattering to me!'

'Oh! I apologize. I didn't mean it quite like that.'

Suddenly her eyes caught him unawares, fixing him with inescapable magnetism.

'I tell you what. You can try just one. Just a tiny experimental one. A sisterly one if you like. If you don't care for it, I'll take the cheque and put the rest away.'

Suddenly she seemed to slide along the seat towards him, at the same time patting one end of it with her hand in invitation.

'Sit,' she said, 'sit,' and he obeyed like a dog.

A moment later a great warm profound cloud of confusion enveloped him. Her lips rested with a light but distinct ardour on his. At the same time she touched his cheek, also lightly, with one hand, and with the other held him firmly by the shoulder, so that there was no chance of his escaping.

The kiss, over in a few seconds, terrified him so much that it might have been of a night's duration. He was about to splutter an expression of something between relief and protest when she laughed and said:

'Oh! you can do better than that. Surely to God you can do better than that.'

In the moment before her arms completely enveloped him he wildly remembered Vanessa La Farge's words about conquest and felt himself to be vainly and desperately struggling against the surge of a waterfall.

This time her lips were loose and sensuous. She moved them caressively, with infinitely gentle compulsion, from side to side. Then to his ultimate horror she grasped one of his hands and lifted it to the curve of her bosom, so that for the first time in his life he found himself incredibly and fearfully aware of the shape of the female breast.

It shattered him so much that he almost wrenched himself away, confusedly protesting, only to find that she was equally unwilling to let him go.

'That was better,' she said. 'That was grand.'

'Miss O'Connor, do you mind, I –'

'I believe you're the dark horse. Vanessa'll be raving jealous when I tell her –'

The ultimate horror of having an embarrassing intimacy crudely exposed to someone else was suddenly more than he could bear. He wrenched himself up from the seat, misjudged his distance, slipped and fell off the end of it.

In a flash, before he had time to attempt to get up, her arms enveloped him. Again her lips took caressive possession of his and again she lifted one of his hands to her breast. How long this shattering experience might have gone on he never knew but a moment or so later a voice shattered him still further:

'Well, there's nothing like getting down to it. Don't mind me.'

Half blindly he started to grope about on his hands and knees, trying to get up. The utter indignity of being discovered by Vanessa La Farge in that compromising attitude was so great that he might actually have been caught in an act of adultery.

'So that's what you two get up to when my back's turned.'

Utterly cool and serene, Kitty O'Connor simply said: 'Nonsense. We were just raising money for charity.'

'I do beg your pardon,' he said. 'I must apologize –'

'Oh! for goodness' sake don't apologize. What on earth is there to apologize about? Some people have all the luck.'

'I just wanted to say that it isn't my usual habit to –'

'Oh! by the way I had a great idea,' she said, coolly too, exactly as if nothing had happened. 'I thought we'd all have a candlelight supper, down here, by the bath-house –'

'Mrs La Farge, I really don't think I could. I really should be going –'

'Oh! but I've already ordered it. Mary's getting it ready. Smoked salmon, cold chicken pie, salad, fresh peaches – how's that? And afterwards we could swim or something.'

'Or something,' Kitty O'Connor said and broke into peals of laughter. 'I like that something.'

'No, no,' he said, 'I really ought to tear myself away.'

Vanessa La Farge laughed too.

'I didn't notice any great effort to tear yourself away just now,' she said, 'if anything quite the contrary.'

'Well, that really wasn't quite what you thought it was.'

'Oh! wasn't it? Really?'

'Inadvertently I –'

'I think I'll go and tidy myself up,' Kitty O'Connor suddenly said, superbly cool too, and again as if nothing had happened. 'What time's supper?'

'Now I really shouldn't stay for supper –'

'Of course you'll stay. We'd love you to stay. We want you to stay. We won't take no for an answer.'

'Mind you behave yourselves while I'm gone,' Kitty O'Connor said and with fresh flute-like scales of laughter went calmly away to the bath-house.

Alone with Vanessa La Farge, he felt himself to be a man sitting on the edge of a volcano.

'I'm very jealous,' she suddenly said.

'Mrs La Farge, this is all very –'

'I'm very jealous.'

Sitting on the stone seat, she seemed to adopt an attitude of extreme petulance, eyeing him covertly, slightly pouting.

'You know, it really wasn't like that –'

'Don't make it worse. You shower kisses on my best friend and then tell me it wasn't like that. It looked pretty well like the real thing to me.'

'It was quite unintentional.'

'Unintentional! But still, as I say, some girls have all the luck. All right, I forgive you. You can make it up to me by going to get me another drink.'

Mute and miserable, he obeyed like a dog.

An hour or more later the flames of four tall green candles fluttered in the slightest evening breeze on the supper table. In between them a vase of sweet-peas, mauve and cream and carmine and maroon and purple, gave off a perfume at once elusive and exotic, causing Vanessa La Farge to say, more than once :

'Ah! the smell of sweet-peas. It always does something to me.'

'Makes you amorous, I expect,' Kitty O'Connor said, 'Like gin does to me.'

'Oh! deeper than that,' she said with mystery, 'much deeper than that.'

The faces of the two women were of great and subtle beauty in the candlelight. To the perfume of sweet-peas and the transcending and mysterious effect they had on Vanessa La Farge was presently added the deeper aroma of peaches ripe from the hot house. And once Vanessa La Farge actually tortured Hartley Wilkinson Spencer still further by taking a peach of perfect substance and holding it against his cheek, delicately rubbing it up and down and then again up and down her own.

'It's one of the most exquisite things ever,' she said, 'the skin of a ripe peach. There's no skin in the world like that.'

Though tortured, he remained impervious beyond the candlelight. As so often happens after sunset the air had grown a little warmer, with only the remotest breath to stir the candle flames. When the meal had reached the stage of dessert Vanessa La Farge again held up a peach to her face, rubbed it slowly against her cheek and then started to peel it, delicately.

'You live alone, Mr Spencer?'

'Well, I have a housekeeper.'

'Ah! Lucky housekeeper.'

Her lips, moist with peach juice, shone as with fresh dew as she smiled slightly and eyed him across the candlelight. Still unmoved, he could only remark :

'She cooks for me, after a fashion. Nothing like your supper tonight, of course.'

'You must come more often.'

After the peaches there was coffee and as the three of them sat sipping it Vanessa La Farge suddenly reached out and took a sweet-pea from the vase. Its petals of deepest maroon seemed to have on them a sheen, delicately gold, borrowed from the candlelight.

'It reminds me of our black magnolia,' she said. 'It has just that same midnight sort of velvet look.'

On the slightly painful subject of the black magnolia he decided to remain silent and she went on :

'The magnolia was a bit of luck. If it hadn't been for that we'd never have met you.'

The teasing in these two simple sentences passed over him like a scrap of summer thistledown floating over a rock.

'Are you sure,' she said, 'you won't change your mind about the fête?'

He couldn't, he said. He simply couldn't. There was a question of a very large contract. It had to be finished in Manchester that very day.

'Oh! fiddlesticks to contracts,' Kitty O'Connor said, 'there's more in life than contracts.'

He smiled at her in pitying silence.

'And me waiting in the little tent,' she said, 'with kisses unlimited.'

The mention of kisses merely seemed to recall his painful behaviour on the seat, before supper, and he seized the moment as a chance to say, looking at his watch :

'I see it's past ten. I ought to be going. My housekeeper will be wondering where I've got to.'

With low ripples of laughter the two women deliberately misinterpreted this remark as having in it something mildly sinister. In a voluptuous voice that was also mocking Kitty O'Connor said:

'I told him he was a dark horse. It doesn't take half an eye to see he's the dark horse.'

Vanessa La Farge held the deep maroon sweet-pea to her face, breathing its perfume, looked across at him with liquid eyes and said:

'Well, we're going to miss you, aren't we, Kitty?'

Holy Mary, they were too, Kitty said.

'Of course I shall send you the cheque –'

'Oh! cheques, cheques,' Vanessa La Farge said, 'anyway who's for a swim?'

Kitty O'Connor accepted the suggestion with delight. Hartley Wilkinson Spencer merely sat silent, indicating refusal. Then Vanessa La Farge said:

'Surely you're not going to refuse us all the time, Mr Spencer? You do swim, don't you?'

'Oh! yes, yes. As a matter of fact I'm tremendously keen on it. I use the pool at the girls' High School every morning. Winter and summer.'

'You never do?' Kitty O'Connor said. 'How interesting.'

'I asked Mary to bring down a pair of trunks when she brought the supper,' Vanessa La Farge said, 'so you can't refuse on that score.'

'Well, it's very kind of you. Just a very quick dip.'

'No hurry,' she said and twirled the dark sweet-pea between her thumb and forefinger, so that it almost seemed to give off sparks in the candlelight, 'the night's still young. One night last week we were swimming until two in the morning.'

'It's so quiet tonight,' Kitty O'Connor said. 'Listen. You can hear the waterfall.'

At last, in this breathless atmosphere on which there seemed also to lie a dark bloom like that on the skin of the peaches and the wings of the sweet-pea flowers, the three of them went off to the bath-house to change. Meticulous, even fussy, with his clothes, he took more than ten minutes to do so and finally emerged in a pair of dark red trunks and a big white towel discreetly round his shoulders.

Five yards from the bath-house door he came to an abrupt halt, as if he had suddenly come up against a wall. The bright candle-flames in front of him had for a moment the effect of separating him from the pool beyond, like footlights in a theatre. His eyes were briefly unable to focus the scene and for a few moments he stood under the disconcerting impression that the nearer edge of the pool was graced with two white statues he had completely failed to notice before.

Then he suddenly realized that these were no less than the figures of Vanessa La Farge and Kitty O'Connor, stripped naked, their full, delicate, rounded backs statuesque and fully revealed in the half darkness.

The slightest movement of Kitty O'Connor's shoulders was enough to make him turn and dash to the bath-house. Even before he reached it he heard the splash of two diving bodies and was mentally putting on his clothes.

Some long time later the two women sat at the table, in the light of the lowering candles, in thick bath-robes, sipping brandy.

'Shall I tell you something?' Vanessa La Farge said.

'What?'

'We failed.'

Their laughter rose and penetrated the fabric of the early summer night like suddenly awakened bird-song.

'I think,' Kitty O'Connor said, 'we tried too hard.'

'Or perhaps, on second thoughts, we don't carry enough ammunition for attacking fortresses.'

Again their laughter, now not only loud but deep-throated and voluptuous, rose on the night air.

'Anyway, how does the song go?' Kitty O'Connor said, ' "it was great fun but it was just one of those things".'

In sudden silence they sat staring at the candlelight. A single dark-bloomed peach still sat in its dish. The deep maroon sweet-pea that Vanessa La Farge once again took from its vase and twirled lightly in her hands, reminding her of the black magnolia, seemed to match it perfectly.

'No, actually,' she said, 'I was thinking of another quotation. Who was it who said "It is better to have loved and lost than never to have loved at all"?'

It was now only Kitty O'Connor's high-spirited pealing laughter that rose to the summer stars.

'Search me,' she said, 'but it certainly wasn't Hartley Wilkinson Spencer.'

Love Me Little, Love Me Long

HE stood looking down the field, across treeless hedges of old hawthorn, away from her. He did not want to look at her face. He felt transfixed by the dead leaves of many primroses in the dyke, burnt to brown skeletons by the drought of summer.

'You could often come over and see us,' she said. 'Come next week. We shall be having a shoot one day.'

'I don't shoot,' he said.

'But you could come over. Now that you live so close again.'

He did not speak. He was thinking of how, in the spring, so many primroses would have been very beautiful all along the dykes, under creamy arches of hawthorn.

'The boys are wonderful shots,' she said. 'Better than their father.'

Now from the rise at the end of the field he could see the farm, clustered cubes of cream stone and straw lying at the end of slopes of pasture, grouped about by coppered chestnut trees.

He looked at his watch.

'You don't have to go,' she said. 'Not yet.'

'I really ought.'

'You come over specially to see me and then before I can bat an eyelid, you're off again. It's hardly fair. After all this time –'

'It was just a call,' he said.

'Yes, but it's hardly fair,' she said. 'I mean –'

She had stopped by the gate and now she was leaning on it, arms triangular on the top bar. She was much bigger, he noticed, than she used to be, the flesh of her neck rather heavy, arms ripe and brown, breasts shapeless and cushioned under thick brown lapels of tweed. But her eyes were still very brilliant, egg-blue and clear, and now, for the first time, they looked straight at him.

'If you must go then promise you'll come over on Tuesday,' she said. 'You can do that.'

'I really ought not –'

'It's so like you,' she said. Her voice was neither sharp nor gentle. 'You start a thing and then half way through you want to give it up.'

He did not know what to say.

'You see, you don't say anything. You know it's true.'

'All right.' He smiled.

'Do you mean all right it's true?' she said, 'or do you mean all right you'll come over?'

He put his hand on the latch of the gate, ready to open it, but she pressed the whole weight of her body against it, defying him, holding it shut. And suddenly he found himself pressed against her, his legs melting across her thighs, one hand still on the cold latch of the gate, the other on her warm neck.

'Oh! God,' she said.

Presently he opened the gate and she did not protest, and he walked across the field in a daze. Bright cloud spilt milkily across the evening sky intensified the low sunlight so that it dazzled him like white fire. He held his hand to his face and suddenly, at the same moment, across the next field, there was the sound of shooting. It startled him so much that he stopped.

'It's the boys,' she said. 'After pigeons.'

She stopped too. For a moment he was going on but she held him back by the arms, turning him round so that her body was flat against him.

'They're awfully good,' she said. 'Pigeons are almost the most difficult thing of all.'

'Are they?'

'Almost.'

She began kissing him as shots rang out again across the field but now she did not seem to notice them and they did not startle him. She kissed him in a series of little gulps, her lips hardened and quick and then suddenly softened across his face hungrily.

'Oh! dear, oh! God,' she said.

He let her go on for a moment longer, not speaking.

'This will never do,' she said. 'It really won't. It will never do.'

He looked at his watch again. This time she did not protest and they began walking across the field again, apart.

'There are wonderful cowslips in this field in the spring,' she said. 'You would like it. You were always the great one for flowers.'

A hundred yards farther on he saw the two boys climbing the stile from the field beyond. She waved her hand and they came across to her. They were hatless, with masses of rather coarse black hair, with lips that seemed too wide and adult for their young faces. He saw that their eyes were blackish and deep and that they were not like her.

The four of them walked towards the farm together and the boys, walking slightly apart with their guns, were stiff and polite, calling him 'Sir' whenever they spoke to him.

Five pigeons flew out from a copse of ash-trees on steely wings and the boys began firing instantly, picking off two with fluent easy shots. There was an adultness about the way they lifted the guns, fired, re-loaded and picked up the fallen birds and he could see that she was very proud.

'Hurry on and tell Nancy that Mr Richardson is staying to supper!' she called.

He suddenly felt that it was a trap, deliberately set for him in the presence of the boys, so that he could not escape it.

'It will be something cold,' she said, 'but there'll be pheasant and we always have a ham. That's one thing about a farm. You never lack for anything.'

'No?' he said, and for the first time she did not answer.

Under the chestnut trees, by the farm, drifts of scorched leaves had been newly blown by wind across the pond in the farmyard, so that they floated there like fleets of brown feathers.

'You would love the chestnuts in spring,' she said. 'There's a pink one too. I think it's that one, there. Yes: it's that one.'

He followed her into the house. He stood in the old respectable farm sitting-room, looking about him at the heavy furniture, the chairs of brown leather, the solid dark chests by the wall, the varnished doors and the skirting boards. It wasn't very prosperous.

She seemed to know what he was thinking and said:

'Excuse me, I must see about the food.'

The elder boy brought him a glass of sherry and then stood in the centre of the room, awkwardly.

'Do you shoot, sir?' he said.

'No.'

The boy was silent for a moment, staring solidly; he seemed not to know what to do or say, and then he said:

'I expect you ride, though, sir, don't you?'

'No,' he said, 'I don't ride.'

They had no more to say to each other and a moment later she came back.

'I've hurried everything up,' she said, 'so that you needn't be late after all. Do you mind if I don't change my dress?'

'No,' he said.

She spoke to the boy:

'Go and wash your hands,' she said. 'And then call your father and tell him supper is ready. And Robert too. Tell him to scrub them well.'

The boy went out of the room.

'They never wash unless you tell them to,' she said.

She suddenly stood rigid, staring at him with glistening hungry blue eyes. She had taken off the coat of her costume. The pale blue of her blouse, cushioned taut by her body, seemed to make the blue of the eyes quite fierce.

'Please come on Tuesday. No, Wednesday. There will be no one here.'

'I —'

'Do come. Please.' She looked round hurriedly and then came back to him, closely, taking hold of his jacket with both hands. 'We could take up where we left off.'

Not speaking or moving, he felt himself listening for the boys to come back. She ran her mouth against his face and he saw beyond her fair head a sudden shoal of chestnut leaves freed from the trees like a wild covey of birds across the pond.

'Do you mind if I kiss you?' she said. 'I have to ask. I have to –'

He put his mouth down to her and then, in the same moment, before he could touch her, he heard the footsteps of the boys coming from the passage outside. She went away from him at once, dragging a hand down his arm, pressing his fingers.

'Did you wash?' she said.

The younger boy, Robert, came first, carrying a glazed tray of birds' eggs. Behind him the elder boy kept the door open with one hand.

'I thought Mr Richardson would like to see my birds' eggs.' The boy smiled.

'Afterwards. After supper,' she said. 'Did you wash?'

'Yes.'

'After supper then. Is your father there?'

'He was in the gun room,' the elder boy said. 'He said he would come.'

'Let me see the eggs,' Richardson said.

'They are very old,' she said. 'They were given him by an uncle. They're not much. Will you have more sherry?'

He said thank you, not looking at her, and walked over to where the boy, holding the birds' eggs, looked like a stolid servant holding out to him a tray of little coloured things to eat.

'Some are old,' the boy said. 'But some are new. Some I collected. Do you know what this is?'

'Isn't it a herring-gull's?'

'I thought so. I was not certain.'

Behind him she called, 'Come and have your sherry before we go in.'

'That's a nightjar's there,' he said. 'That's good.'

'Yes, I collected them. That's mine –'

'Put them away now,' his mother said. 'There will be plenty of time afterwards. Or another day.'

The boy was pained but she did not see it. She seemed to be caught up in a tenuous moment of suspense, rigid and oblivious, somewhere between the glass of sherry she was holding and Richardson's eyes.

Then from the door the elder boy said :

'Here's father now. Just coming.'

He took the glass of sherry from her and turned, and it was as if, by the door, the elder boy had grown suddenly to a man of forty. The father, stocky, broad and weathered, with the same coarse dark hair, stood there, rubbing together large hairy brown hands.

'You're just in time. We can go in,' she said. She was very nervous; she said something in a dazed way about forgetting the introductions.

'No need, no need,' the father said. 'We'll dispense with formalities.' He shook hands with Richardson, the stocky hand muscular and warm. 'Which way did you go?'

'We walked across the cowslip field,' she said.

'See any birds?'

'No. Robbie, put away the eggs now. No, there was nothing,' she said.

'It's a bad season. It's something terrible,' he said.

The boy put the tray of eggs on the table and then the five of them went out of the room, across the passage and into the dining-room beyond, for supper. It was twilight in the dining-room because of the shadow of a walnut-tree, still green, on that side of the house, and one of the boys switched on the light above the table.

On the table was a ham on a pink dish, with a brace of cold pheasants beside it and bread and salad and several large pieces of butter, with bottles of beer. At the head of the table the father sliced the ham steadily and thickly and dissected the pheasants and one of the boys poured the beer.

She did not speak and they began eating. Richardson, for

something to say, spoke of the weather and the father said how hot and dry the summer had been and how terribly bad it was for the birds.

'It's very bad,' he said several times. 'Absolutely awful. There'll be no birds at all.'

Richardson did not know what to say. 'Of course it's been quite exceptional,' he said. 'What about partridges?'

'As wild as blazes. You can't get near them. It's somethng terrible. I don't know what we're going to do.'

Richardson ate in silence and listened to the sound, across the farmyard, of the falling wind in the dying chestnut leaves. The evening was very beautiful, the sky electric blue under the dark walnut leaves, and he heard a solitary pheasant crying from across the fields.

The father took a deep drink of beer and said:

'How do you find the ham?'

'Delicious,' he said. 'Wonderfully good.'

'One of our own.' the father said. 'At least we've always got that. At least we can feed.'

'You see, I told you,' she said.

Richardson turned sharply at the sound of her voice from the bottom of the table. She looked at him in a moment of glittering calm, but the glance was unsustained. She could not look at him any longer.

Her eyes were terribly and hungrily blue and the pheasant cried again across the fields and he was transfixed by a fragmentary moment of pain.

'You see, I told you. We never lack for anything here. We have everything we want,' she said.

Same Time, Same Place

ONE had to keep up appearances, Miss Treadwell always told herself. Whatever else happened one simply had to keep up appearances. After all one had one's pride.

The sepia musquash coat she always wore throughout the winter had not only the advantage of keeping her warm and making her look almost of upper middle class but of also concealing the fact that underneath it she wore a man's woollen cardigan and a brown imitation leather waistcoat picked up for a shilling at a rummage sale. Underneath these garments her corsets had so far fallen to pieces that every now and then she padded them with folds of newspaper. If these failed to give her buxom but not too ample figure the distinguished and elegant line she saw so often in advertisements they at least were warm too and cheap and comforting. Above all they helped to keep up appearances.

Miss Treadwell, who was in her late fifties, was apt to refer to her minute bed-sitter, a mere dog kennel, seven feet by ten, as 'my little domain', though if occasion demanded she might enlarge a little on that, calling it 'my apartment'. A divan bed, a chair, a table and a sink left no room whatever for a cooker, though this hardly mattered, since she never cooked except to make toast over a gas-ring. Her diet consisted mostly, except on Sundays, of bread, margarine and tea, though even this, for various reasons, she only had occasionally at home.

Every morning, at about eleven o'clock, she went out and sat on one of the seats in the public gardens. One didn't have to wait long there before someone dropped a newspaper into a litter basket, so that one got the news of the day for nothing besides a new padding for the corsets when necessary. After reading for another half hour Miss Treadwell then went into a small café round the corner and had her lunch. This too con-sisted of a bread roll, margarine and a pot of tea.

It was most important always to order a pot of tea, since in this way one got a small basin of cube sugar, most of which was easily slipped into a hand-bag. It was also important to select a table where someone else had recently been eating. In this way one quite often found two or three pennies or even sixpence left under a plate and uncollected by a busy waitress.

Afte lunch she always went back to the gardens to visit the *Public Ladies*. It was quite extraordinary what one sometimes found in the *Public Ladies*. Frequently someone had forgotten a lipstick, a powder compact, a comb, a box of eye-shadow. Once Miss Treadwell had actually found a small handbag con-taining, among other things, a bottle of peroxide. With the use of this she suddenly went sensationally and almost youthfully blonde, thus keeping up appearances dramatically.

She had learnt other tricks by experience: for example that late on Saturday afternoons one could buy, for a few pence, bags of unsold cakes that wouldn't keep in the shops until Mon-day, or bags of broken biscuits which made a delicious Sunday treat if you put them in a basin and poured a layer of thin hot chocolate over them. There were also flowers: sometimes as you walked through the street market you came across a whole box of them, daffodils or roses or carnations or gladioli, that had dropped from a lorry and nobody had ever bothered to pick up. A few swiftly snatched up stalks turned the kennel-like bed-sitter into a little paradise.

Soon after the incident of the peroxide, that had turned her a light youthful blonde and helped to keep up her appearances so dramatically, she was sitting in the public gardens on an April morning. The day was suddenly and unusually hot; tulips that had been mere half-green buds the day before were now becoming, every moment, more and more like shimmering open wine glasses of pink and scarlet and yellow; an occasional white or yellow butterfly skimmed through the many wide yellow trumpets of daffodils under trembling pink canopies of cherry blossom. All the many seats in the gardens were crowded. It was very much a morning when appearances mattered.

The only place she could find to sit down was next to a gentleman who, because of the sudden April heat, had taken off his black homburg hat and laid it on the seat beside him. As Miss Treadwell approached he removed the hat and balanced it on his knee. His hair was a smooth iron grey. This alone would not have confirmed him as a gentleman but the homburg hat most certainly did. Men who wore homburg hats were always gentlemen.

After studying his newspaper in concentrated silence for another five minutes he folded it up and laid that too on the seat beside him. Unwilling to appear too eager Miss Treadwell waited some further minutes before saying:

'I hope you won't think me rude but I wonder – could I take a tiny glance at your newspaper? I couldn't get one this morning.'

'Oh! by all means. By all means. Take it, please. I've finished with it anyway.'

'Oh! I didn't mean to take it altogether.'

'Oh! do. I've finished the cross-word. And once I've finished that I'm not interested. Do you do the cross-word?'

No, Miss Treadwell had to confess, she never did the cross-word. She supposed she wasn't clever enough for that.

'Nor was I, this morning. There was a devil of a clue and the only word that fitted was *poitivene*. Had me stuck for an hour. Do you know what a *poitivene* is?'

Miss Treadwell suddenly felt flattered and very pleased with herself. Yes, she said, as a matter of fact she did.

'And what on earth is it?'

'It's a sort of chrysanthemum.'

'Is it by Jove? How ever did you know?'

Miss Treadwell said she had seen them on the market flower stalls, named. There was another one called *rayonante*. She always thought they were such pretty names, she said, and the gentleman in the homburg hat gave her a long friendly blue-eyed stare of admiration.

Silence came between them for some few minutes after this, until finally the gentleman in the homburg hat said:

'What a beautiful morning.'

'Lovely. Spring at last.'

'Spring at last.'

Miss Treadwell now opened the paper and pretended to read it without actually seeing a single word. At the same time the gentleman in the homburg hat extended a hand and laid it on the paper and said:

'The cartoon's rather good today. Page five. Allow me.'

As the gentleman in the homburg hat turned the pages of the paper over Miss Treadwell suddenly noticed an extraordinary thing. On the third finger of his left hand he was wearing a rather large ring. It was in the shape of a turquoise butterfly set in a clear white stone.

With considerable diffidence Miss Treadwell said:

'What a most unusual ring, if you forgive me for saying so.'

'It is rather unusual.'

The gentleman in the homburg hat held out the ring for her to look at more closely. She gazed at it for some seconds and then said:

'It looks sort of Chinese.'

'Indian, I'm told.'

'Is it a sort of charm, a good luck thing or something?'

'Sort of. The butterfly is supposed to represent summer and the white stone winter and ice and all that. I suppose it's a sort of symbol of the resurgence of spring over winter. Well, so I've been told.'

Miss Treadwell could only listen in fervent, silent admiration. The stone flashed in the sun. And was it sort of lucky? she said.

'Supposed to be. But I'm afraid this thing has produced more than its fair share of trouble.'

'Oh! how could that be?'

'It belonged to my eldest sister. She left it to me. Consequently my other sister – I live with her – has never forgiven her. She gives me hell about it.'

Miss Treadwell fell into a depressive silence, not knowing what to say. The silence lasted several minutes until at last he said:

'Still, I suppose I ought to be thankful she looks after me. Do you live near by?'

'My apartment is just round the corner.'

'You live alone?'

'Oh! quite.'

'In a way I envy you. At least you've no one to quarrel with. Every day I'm glad when breakfast is over. Then I can be off on my own.'

In silence Miss Treadwell again gazed at the butterfly imprisoned in its ice.

'Do you find it difficult to fill in the day?' the man in the homburg hat said.

'Oh! no, no, no. It's terribly, terribly full. By the time I've done my cooking and cleared up the apartment and so on the time simply flies. I do a lot of flower arrangement.'

'I find it hangs like hell.'

They sat for some time longer in the sun, without speaking. Then the man in the homburg hat looked at his pocket watch and said:

'Well, I fear I must be going; we always have lunch at dead on twelve. If I'm not there she starts creating like fury.'

'I must be going too,' Miss Treadwell said. 'I've my own lunch to get. And then I'm making new curtains for the sitting-room.'

'Ah! you're clever at that sort of thing?'

'Oh! I don't know about clever. As a matter of fact I don't think I am. I sort of mis-measured the windows and now I need yards and yards more material.'

'I suppose that's the trouble with large windows.'

'Yes. Yes. However, we shall get over it. I know they have plenty more at the shop.'

The man in the homburg hat got up, put on his hat and then took it off again in a courteous gesture.

'Well, good-bye. It's been so nice to meet you. Oh! by the way my name is Thornhill.'

The butterfly imprisoned in its ice flashed in the sun.

'And you, Mr Thornhill.'

*

After that they began to meet at more or less the same spot, at more or less the same time, on most week-days. The weather continued warm, sometimes even hot, and Miss Treadwell discarded the musquash coat and some of the newspaper under it, wearing instead a pale pink jersey dress and a pair of brown imitation crocodile shoes she had picked up for a shilling or two at a rummage sale.

'I'm feeling rather affluent today,' was the first remark with which Mr Thornhill greeted Miss Treadwell one morning. They had been meeting for nearly a month now.

'Oh? Why is that?'

'I've started to draw my pension.' He laughed, rather against himself, pleasantly. 'I think it's rather funny. Do you have the pension yet?'

Oh! no, no, dear me no, Miss Treadwell said. She laughed too. Did he mind? She hadn't quite got as far as that yet. All in good time.

'Earlier in life one tends to rather despise the thought. And when the time comes it's rather nice. Well, I expect you won't be too proud to take it when it arrives?'

'Well, of course luckily I have private means.' It was a lie, but one had to keep up appearances. Miss Treadwell's means consisted of a small Post Office Savings Account from which she extracted a minute sum every Monday morning. 'I simply couldn't manage the apartment without.'

'Those curtains must have cost you a bit.'

'Oh! the earth. The absolute earth.'

'On the subject of affluence,' he suddenly said, 'I feel in honour bound to buy you a drink this morning. Would you?'

'But it's only half past eleven –'

'By the time we've walked to *The Lansdowne Arms* it'll be twelve o'clock.'

'*The Lansdowne Arms* –'

Miss Treadwell, who couldn't afford to drink anyway, suddenly found herself confronted with impossible visions of grandeur and felt slightly frightened. Walking across the public gardens she kept her hands tightly folded in front of her, in case one or more of the newspapers should slip and fall down.

In the bar of *The Lansdowne Arms* all was wrapped in a red, subdued light. Like scarlet torches a great base of gladioli flamed on the bar.

'Now name it,' Mr Thornhill said. 'Anything you like. After all it isn't every day a man becomes of age. Sherry, port, gin, whisky, beer? – what shall it be?'

Miss Treadwell hesitatingly confessed that she felt ever so slightly tempted towards a small sherry.

'Splendid. I'll have a sherry too. But a dry one. And make them,' he said to the waiting barman, 'large ones.'

Sherry in hand, Miss Treadwell sat bathed in dreams of grandeur that, for all their emergence into reality, were now more impossible than ever. The sherry warmed her throat, crawled snakily through her empty stomach and moistened her eyes. Mr Thornhill said 'cheers' several times and then suddenly burst out laughing.

'God, I wish my sister could see me now.'

He positively swigged at his sherry while Miss Treadwell gently sipped at hers.

'Hell. Why do the children of the same parents so often hate each other?'

To this question, almost barked out, Miss Treadwell had no answer and simply went on sipping her sherry.

'Some days the atmosphere in that house is poisonous. We hiss at each other like two snakes. One day –'

Miss Treadwell started to think up what seemed at first a presumptuous remark but another sip or two of sherry finally fortified her to make it.

'Perhaps if you gave her the ring it might help things –'

'Good God, what? Can't you just hear her? – "Oh! far be it from me to take the ring from you. If Alice had wished me to have the ring she would have left it to me. But the fact is she didn't, did she? Oh! no it's your ring. Not all the wild dogs in China" – that's one of her favourite maddening expressions, "all the wild dogs in China" –'

Mr Thornhill savagely drained his sherry glass.

'Have you ever known what it is to want to murder some-body?'

Oh! dear me no, Miss Treadwell said, her voice barely audible. Oh! dear me –

'It's not funny,' Mr Thornhill said. 'It's not funny. Still, drink up. Second round. This is the day.'

Miss Treadwell started meekly to protest that really one was enough for her, but Mr Thornhill was already waving an expansive arm in the direction of the bar.

'Well, if you insist,' Miss Treadwell said, 'but only a very small one this time –'

Of course he insisted, Mr Thornhill said and snapped out the words 'Same again, barman,' only to retract them a second later.

'No, make mine whisky. A double Black-and-White.'

His sister didn't drink either, he went on to say. That made her sub-human for a start. A good drink now and then did a lot to make a person human, didn't Miss Treadwell agree?

The barman having brought the new drinks Mr Thornhill drank gaspily at his whisky, confessing that sherry really wasn't his tipple. With whisky a man had something. It – what did they say nowadays? – it sent you.

'We must do this more often. Make it an every morning thing.'

Mr Thornhill, having drunk half his whisky neat, now poured a little water into the rest of it, complaining at the same time that you didn't get much of a measure nowadays. In no time you were ready for another.

'By the way, did you finish your curtains?'

No, Miss Treadwell had to confess, she hadn't yet.

'Well, promise me something. When you do, invite me up to see them. Fair enough? I envy you that apartment of yours. I really envy you. God, it would be nice to live on one's own – Well, promise me?'

Well, it would be some time yet, Miss Treadwell found herself saying. Inwardly she trembled with cold apprehension. There had been some hitch about the material. The stock of the original yellow had run out and she hadn't been able to match it up.

'Well, all in good time. All in good time. But promise me?'

After a third large whisky Mr Thornhill gave the distinct impression of talking through a muslin bag. The folds of his neck were perceptibly reddened. From time to time he locked and unlocked the fingers of his two hands and finally, in one of these unsteady gestures, he took off the butterfly ring. To her infinite and tortured astonishment Miss Treadwell suddenly heard the words:

'You said something about giving the ring back to Beryl. Well, blast Beryl. I want to give it to you. Get what I mean?' He held out the bright imprisoned butterfly. 'Go on. Take it. Slip it on.'

'Mr Thornhill, I don't quite understand –'

'Go on. Third finger, left hand.'

The butterfly imprisoned in its ice sparkled. Miss Treadwell proceeded to lift her glass of sherry, only to find herself trembling so much that she had to set it down again. Mr Thornhill smacked the palms of his hands together and his voice was over-loud.

'You get what I'm asking you, don't you? It isn't always easy to say these things.'

Half-terrified, Miss Treadwell made yet another attempt to lift her glass of sherry. This time she managed to get it to her lips, spilling much of it down her chin. As she mopped at it with her handkerchief it appeared to Mr Thornhill that she might have been about to cry. She did in fact feel like crying and sat for some moments biting her lips hard, locked in impotent nervous distress.

'Well,' Mr Thornhill said. 'What say you? Do you know, I don't even know your Christian name.'

'Doris.'

Mr Thornhill laughed tipsily.

'Doris, I'm asking you – yes, I know – I expect you're going to say "this is all so sudden" –'

Well, it was, sort of, Miss Treadwell said. A vision of her bed-sitter, the dog-kennel, suddenly rose up to mock her. The loud plop of the gas-ring as she lit it echoed through her mind, extinguishing for a moment every thought. Again the imprisoned butterfly sparkled. A moment later, unsteadily grabbing at his glass, Mr Thornhill dropped the ring on the floor.

Picking it up, he was visibly trembling too.

'I thought perhaps we could both manage in your apartment – with my pension and your – unless perhaps you'd prefer to be independent –'

Desperately, as never before in her life, Miss Treadwell sought to keep up appearances by taking her powder compact from her bag, looking into its mirror and slowly powdering her nose. The face she saw in the glass, pallid and stiff, seemed not to belong to her and hastily she shut the compact down.

'Well, what do you say?'

'I don't know what – well, anyway not today, Mr Thornhill. Please, not today.'

'Not Mister Thornhill. Harry. Tomorrow then? Same time, same place, tomorrow. Here.'

'I think I ought to go now, Mr Thornhill.'

'Harry, Harry please. Go, my foot. I'm going to have another whisky.' Mr Thornhill's command of 'Same again' was so sharp and loud that a wire-haired terrier belonging to a tweeded gentleman at the far end of the bar yapped out a series of loud and agitated barks. In its feverish agitation it might well have been the echo of the voice of Miss Treadwell pleading for some sort of escape or mercy.

'Good-bye,' she said. 'I really must go.' Her voice was in fact barely audible. 'Good-bye – I really must go now –'

'Don't forget.' Mr Thornhill staggered unsteadily to his feet, eyes watering weakly, the imprisoned butterfly flashing again as he sought to shake her hand. 'Same time, same place –'

After that Miss Treadwell never sat in the public gardens again. She now goes, instead, to a park half a mile away. In the park is a small lake. In the centre of the lake is an island covered with low shrubbery and a number of wooden coops where ornamental water-birds, bright mallards, unusual geese and even moorhens can shelter.

Every morning Miss Treadwell, struggling always, with pride, to keep up appearances, takes with her a small bag of stale cakes or broken biscuits and throws them to the birds and then persuades herself it is sort of fun to watch which ones, greedy and squabbling, grab the biggest pieces first.

'Tomorrow,' she always tells herself, 'Same time, same place.' She also reads the newspaper.

The Middle of Nowhere

WHEN Francie Williams's husband died of acute alcoholism at the age of thirty-two nobody wept, least of all Francie.

Williams had been a big swaggering man of almost alarmingly handsome physique, with rippling black hair that looked almost muscular, a remarkable capacity for indolence and liquor and an ungovernable violent temper. He had started his working life as a motor mechanic, found it altogether too exhausting and had drifted into running a so-called filling and service station ten miles from the North Sea coast – so-called because there was no filling unless Francie did it and no service because no mechanic could ever be found to put up with the indolence, the drink and the ungovernable temper for more than a week or two.

At the point where the station stood the land had the appearance of being crudely carved out of scoured grey bone. Most of the fields were flat, open and without hedges. Nearer the coast the soil changed to an arid bed of shale and shingle, populated only by grey whining gulls. One of the many reasons Williams had continually advanced as the cause of the run-down of the filling station was the winter wind of razor bitterness that blew in almost ceaselessly from the sea, bringing snow when other parts were free of it and bending and blistering the few trees into dark contortions in its wrathful fury. Another was the isolation.

'It's like living in the middle of nowhere. In the middle of bloody nowhere.'

Still another reason was that some day, at some unspecified date, a new trunk road was to be driven down to the coast, two hundred yards from the garage, thus diverting traffic and making all thoughts of improvements and even maintenance a hopeless waste of time.

157

So a dump of rusting car-wrecks, old oil drums, obsolete break-down gear and black mountains of discarded tyres grew up about the place, half-obliterating it. A gale of exceptional fury blew down the one match-wood repair shop, scattering its corrugated roof into a field beyond. The concrete apron about the filling pumps cracked like a jig-saw puzzle, sprouting weeds. An air of desertion crept over and finally gripped the place, so that nine out of every ten drivers passed it without a second look, believing it dead. For the few who did stop Francie gave the only service that any longer existed : petrol, oil, air and where you could get the nearest decent cup of tea or coffee. Even that was four miles down the road.

Francie, at twenty-nine, was big too. She was one of those women, fair, steamy-eyed, generous of mouth and with a girth of thigh that recalled a brood mare, who matures at a sensationally early age and often by thirty decays into fat and sloppiness, half run to seed. But at the time Williams died her skin still had on it the bloom you see on a plum at the height of its ripeness and there was still a deceptive, smouldering, steamy light in the pair of big violet eyes that were really extraordinarily tender.

Williams had been dead three months or so when a brand new Mini estate car drew up one afternoon at the pump with a middle-aged man and his wife inside. The man asked for four gallons of petrol and then, jumping out of the car, started fussing over it with a yellow duster like an over-zealous hen with an only surviving chick.

'Serve teas here?' he said and Francie said no, she was afraid she didn't, but they would get some at *The Blue Schooner Café*, a few miles down the road.

'We passed that. Seems to be closed. Looked as if they might have had a bit of a fire.'

Francie said it was the first she'd heard of it and the man gave a big thirsty sigh, almost gasping at the warmth of the July afternoon.

'Couldn't manage us a cup, I suppose?' he said. 'Dying for one. I think it's the salt in the air.'

Well, she supposed she might, Francie said. She generally made herself one about this time of day.

Ten minutes later she was carrying a tray of tea out to the car. With the tea was the only thing she could find in the kitchen to eat: half a cold Cornish pasty left over from her lunch and which she had now cut up into neat, narrow fingers.

Almost at once the man went into a state of near-poetical rapture about the pasty. He had never tasted anything quite so good in all his natural. The pastry melted away in the mouth like butter. The meat, the whole thing, was a dream. Did he assume it was of her own making?

Well, yes, Francie admitted, it was. She didn't ever think of it as anything all that special though.

'You should open a place here,' the man said. 'Start a *café*. There's a big call for a place like that along here. You could make a bomb.'

'Some hopes,' Francie said. 'Me? I've only got one pair of hands.'

The incident passed completely from her mind, never prompting another thought, and might have remained thus utterly forgotten if it hadn't been for a second one a few days later.

On a warm salt-laden morning of brisk wind she had just finished serving a baker's delivery van with half a dozen gallons of petrol when she turned to see, on the concrete apron, a small dark man of about forty staring at her. He seemed suddenly to have dropped in from nowhere.

Black hair, black eyebrows and mild brilliant blue eyes gave his face an air of strangely innocent illumination. But these were by no means the most arresting things about him, The most remarkable thing about him was that in one hand he was carrying a bunch of wayside flowers, already drooping in the sun, and in the other a parcel of newspaper from one end of which protruded the gaping curious heads of three or four fresh herrings.

'Good morning,' he said, 'any kind of work around this place?'

Something about the flowers and the fish had the effect of inducing in Francie first a desire to laugh and then to cry. His voice, like his face, was bland with an altogether disarming innocence. Not knowing quite what to say she simply stood there, staring at the flowers.

He lifted them up. 'All sea flowers. That's a sea poppy.' The sea poppy was pale yellow. 'This is a bit of sea thistle.' The sea thistle was as blue and sharp as steel. 'I gathered them coming in from the coast. I'll do any kind of work.'

His eyes wandered across the cracked concrete apron, over the piles of rusting junk and the gale-battered repair shed.

'What happened to the shed?'

'A gale –'

'I'll clean the drains.'

'I don't know that they want cleaning.'

'You want the roof put back on the shed? I'll have a go at the shed.'

Irresistibly the innocence of the blue eyes held her uneasily captivated. Then suddenly he held out both fish and flowers. Would she like the herrings? They were fresh. He'd bought them straight from a man with a boat. He had soles too.

'Let me have a go at the shed.'

Between that moment and the end of the long light summer evening he worked, single-handed, and put the roof back on the shed. As the light faded seawards into a breathless sky, half green, half-apricot, she thanked him and asked him what she owed him now.

'Give me somewhere to doss and we'll call it quits.'

'Oh! that's not fair. I've got no room anyway.'

There was an old Chrysler limousine behind the shed, he told her. It was still good inside. He could doss in that.

Just as she had agreed to take fish and flowers and let him

work on the shed, almost against her will, she now agreed to the impossible notion of his sleeping in the limousine.

'You'll need a blanket or two,' she said and went into the house to get some.

Coming back with the blankets, some minutes later, she observed him walking from the direction of the shed. All day she had noticed the lightness of his walk. His feet, like his hands, were very small. While not actually dancing across the concrete he appeared to be lightly blown along. And once again she found herself afflicted with the impossible impulse to laugh and then to cry.

'Where are you making for, anyway?' she said.

'I've been working with a pipe-laying gang. Contract work. The money was good but I suddenly had a fancy to take a month or two off. I'm making for Liverpool.'

'Are you a Liverpool man?'

'No. Irish. From Ulster.'

'You're not walking there?'

'Yes, I'm walking.'

'That's a long, long way.'

'I've all the time in the world,' he said. 'All the time in the world.'

Before turning in to sleep in the limousine he said, 'I'll clean out the shed tomorrow and then later in the week –' an assumption of permanence that presently began to be repeated from day to day. Tomorrow he would do this, the next day that, and irresistibly Francie drifted into letting him stay.

Almost a week later an elderly couple drew up one afternoon in a car. They were friends of the people who had heaped their almost celestial praise on the Cornish pasty. They had come to sample it themselves.

Francie was sorry : there was no Cornish pasty. Disappointed, the couple urged that she should do something about this regretful state of affairs. There was, they were convinced, a great opening for a *café* here. You couldn't get a cup of tea along the whole ten miles to the coast.

'Get me another dozen pairs of hands,' Francie said.

The small, light-footed man stood listening.

'Well, you've got four,' he said.

'How's that?'

'Mine and yours. I could fit the shed up as a *café*. Easy. I'll paint a sign. A good big one.'

Once more she drifted into acquiescence. Within a week the sign – *TEAS – CAFÉ – SNACKS* – was painted, broad and high in white and green. At an auction sale down on the coast she bought a quantity of second-hand tables and chairs, cutlery and crocks. She acquired two vast brown teapots and discovered within herself an untapped capacity for lightness in cooking. She began to turn out not merely the celestial Cornish pasties but meat pies, sausage rolls, currant buns, fruit cakes, tarts, sandwiches, hot dogs.

In the way that news of such things spreads she presently found that anything up to ten heavy lorries might be parked on the concrete apron at midday and even more between four and six in the evening. Soon she was confronted with an insatiable demand for bacon and eggs, bacon and chips, egg and chips, fish fingers and chips. She acquired more crocks and cutlery, hired a larger brand-new electric stove. The young wife of a farm labourer from down the road began to come in to help and then brought her sister too.

It presently began to be clear that many drivers were drawing up not merely to sample Francie's cooking but on the chance, if possible, of sampling Francie herself. Many remembered Williams; not a few were quick to notice that far from shrouding herself in lamentation for the departed handsome alcoholic she appeared rather to have flowered. She was stupefyingly mature but still young, physically more immensely desirable than ever, and to not a single one of them did it ever occur why.

It appeared to the greater part of them that she was what men called easy meat. Such a body had clearly been created from more than mere admiration from afar off. It was a feast of flesh. There appeared a sudden crop of wives who didn't understand their husbands, of drivers tormented with the woman-less darkness of long night distances, of drivers who wanted a bed, and if possible Francie's bed, for the night.

Not one of them had the slightest persuasive effect on her. If the big expansive body appeared to be outwardly promis-cuous, warm to a point of steaminess, the inner woman re-mained cool, withdrawn, even frigid. To not one of them, for some long time, did it ever remotely occur that she might have her own secluded source of devotion.

By August of that year the little light-stepped man, whose name now turned out to be Brady and who had first brought fish and flowers and who still slept in the old Chrysler limou-sine, had dug up a fairly large patch of ground at the back of the *café* and had planted it with potatoes, onions, carrots, beans and lettuces and, at one end, a few rows of larkspur, cornflowers and marigolds. Sometimes in the evenings she stole ten minutes or so from the greasy heat of the *café* and went out for a breath of fresh air, watching him dig or hoe. Never once did the extraordinary lightness of his movements fail to induce in her the strangest waves of excitement, rising always to that same almost unbearable desire to laugh or cry.

On a particularly busy evening towards the end of that month, with the *café* full of men guzzling tea and scooping up chips in every form, Brady suddenly came in with a bunch of marigolds and larkspur. They were merely for the purpose of decorating the *café* counter but something about the way he held them straight out in front of him, like a rather ashamed supplicant seeking to beg some sort of forgiveness, had about it that air of innocence that to her was always so touching but that now, in public, seemed to verge almost on the ridiculous.

Throughout the *café* there were several seconds of utter silence and then every man began laughing.

A wave of white-hot anger swept through Francie. She picked up a cup and promptly dropped it. An impossible, impassioned impulse to pick up a knife and drive it into someone leapt through her, died and left her coldly sweating. In another spasm of silence, after the laughter had spent itself, she incredibly heard the word 'Billikins', never once dreaming or discovering until later that this was the mocking little name by which every man now knew Brady.

She consciously knew then, for the first time, that she was in love with him. She knew too that it wasn't merely a possessive or obsessive love but a highly imperative one. There was revealed inside her not only an immeasurable depth of tenderness but an even greater cavern of hunger waiting to be satisfied.

It was quite dark when she finally shut the *café*, slipped on a dressing gown and went over to the old Chrysler limousine. The back windows of the car were wound down but she tapped gently on the door and asked was he asleep, was she disturbing him?

'No,' he said. 'I'm awake.'

Might she come in?

'Yes,' he said. 'Come in.'

She opened the car door and climbed into the back. He moved along the wide plush seat to give her room to sit down. Insufferably nervous, she tried to put into her voice a note that was casual:

'It's a warm evening. I thought I must get myself a breath of fresh air.'

'It's warm. Yes. It is that.'

For some moments longer she had nothing more to say. She stared through the windows of the car at a sky that, seawards, still carried the faintest white glow above the horizon, with an early star or two hanging above.

'You were extra busy tonight,' he said.

'I'm sorry about what happened. About the flowers.'

'It did nothing to worry me.'

'It did to me. I don't like a man to be laughed at.'

'I say it did nothing to worry me. You know how the fellers are.'

His voice, very soft and disembodied in the darkness, seemed to intensify every moment with an air of great intimacy. She found her own voice lowering itself too.

'You've been here two months now.'

'Like I say, I've all the time in the world.'

'It'll soon be getting too cold to sleep in this thing.'

He laughed very quietly. 'I can always get myself a hot water bottle.'

Something about this quiet laugh stirred her deeply. Without conscious impulse she stretched out her right hand until she could feel one of his in the darkness. The small fingers were surprisingly cool on so warm an evening and her own started tingling sharply at the moment of contact. This tingling presently started running down through her body. Her legs quivered. A hot flush of excitement made her impulsively throw back the lapels of her dressing gown and a second later she stretched out both hands.

'Where are you?' she said. 'I can't see you in the dark.'

Unbearably excited, she caught his two hands.

'Feel of me,' she said. 'Feel of me –'

The innocence in him that she had so often found impossibly touching now kept his hands rigidly suspended, some distance away from her, the fingers half-clenched. She let them remain like that for some seconds longer and then, as it were, un-locked them and started to guide them towards her big breasts.

Even when the small cool fingers touched her warm skin there still seemed to be an enormous innocent reluctance in him. For some moments she waited in vain for some caressive movement of his fingers against her breasts but they still re-mained rigid and suspended and at last she said :

'You're not afraid of anything, are you? You're surely not afraid of me?'

Amazingly the fingers slowly relaxed, drawing her breasts together and then letting them part again. The gesture prompted in her a great rush of emotion, so that she suddenly leaned forward and pressed her open lips against his face.

'There's no need to sleep here any longer.'

He said nothing and again the often repeated impulse to laugh and then to cry ran through her, this time taking her near to tears.

'Don't go away from me, will you?' she said. 'Ever. Don't ever go away from me.'

From then onwards he slept in her bed and for the next two months or so she became the victim of a deep delusion. It was that what went on between Brady and herself was an affair of utter secrecy.

What she didn't know, at least for some time, was that it was a means of common gossip, common fun, to every driver who ever pulled up at the *café*. Brady himself, small, light of step, soft spoken, was himself a figure of some inadequacy, even slight ridicule. Set beside the big voluptuous steamy-eyed figure of Francie he became the easy, obvious, contemptible joke.

'Billikins the Lover Boy', they all called him. 'Francie's Fancy'.

All this might have gone on for much longer if it hadn't been for an incident early in September. Dusk was just falling one sultry evening when she saw from the windows of the *café* a green three-ton lorry pull up at the pumps outside and the driver, alighting from it, go straight to the air pump and begin to check his tyres.

More curious than annoyed, she went out and found a driver she had never seen before, a big, dark-haired, muscular man of thirty or so, rather of Williams' swaggering build, with longish side-linings, whistling with a cocky sort of air as he moved from tyre to tyre.

'Help yourself,' she said. 'Don't bother to ask.'

'Always help myself first, duckie, and ask afterwards.'

'Perhaps you'd like to help yourself to petrol? All free of course.'

'All right for petrol, duckie. Just the air.'

She felt herself bristling. Cockily whistling again, he made the air tube dance and coil about the back of the lorry like a long thin snake.

A second later she could have sworn that there was a warm ripe smell of strawberries in the air.

'Right first time, duckie. Got a couple o' ton aboard.'

Strawberries in September? She'd never heard of strawberries in September.

'Well, you've heard now.' He lifted the green tarpaulin canopy at the back of the lorry, revealing in the half light trays of fat scarlet strawberries stacked high. 'Second crop. You set fire to the fields as soon as the first crop's finished and if the weather's right you make a bomb in September.

'Try one?'

With that cocky air of his he picked up a strawberry of luscious ripeness and size, held it by the stalk and actually pressed it against her lips. The sweetness of the berry caused her to give an involutary gasp of pleasure. The exuding juice ran down her chin.

'Pretty good flavour, eh?'

'Marvellous.'

'Take a tray.'

'Oh! I couldn't do that, thanks all the same —'

'Plenty more where they came from, duckie.' Already he was reaching inside the lorry to take a tray of strawberries down. 'Always sling a few extra on board. Where will I put them?'

Quite without thinking she said 'Better put them in my sitting-room. If they see them in the *café* there'll be a riot.'

He carried the tray of strawberries into her sitting-room. It was still not quite dark. The warm fragrance of strawberries was rich on the air. Cockily he picked out a berry even larger than the first, bit into it and then held out the remainder, pressing it against her lips.

The intimacy of the moment took her by surprise. A second later his hand was exploring the curve of her breast.

'Do you take everything for free?' she said.

'They always say the best things in life are, duckie.'

'Well, you're pretty free with your hands, I'll say that.'

She tried to remove his hand from her breast. He merely clasped it more closely.

'Married?'

'I don't suppose it would make the slightest difference to you if I was.'

'I always say you're all the same shape, duckie. Only you happen to be a better shape than most.'

'Take your hand away, I run a *café* here. Not a –'

'I fancy you.'

'Well, you'll fancy on, that's all.'

He made a clumsy, brutish sort of attempt to kiss her. She was sensible enough not to smack his face but merely said, coldly:

'You pick women like you pick strawberries, I suppose?'

'Just about, duckie. Pick 'em up and lay 'em down, that's me.'

'Excuse me. I'm going. I run a *café* here, I tell you. I've got customers –'

'Always a customer here, duckie. Any time.'

'Do you mind not mauling me?'

She broke away and started to walk to the door. He laughed.

'I'll be by tomorrow night and every night till the crop's finished,' he said. 'There'll be a tray for you whenever you want one.'

'Thanks. I never eat too many strawberries. They bring me out in a rash.'

'Really, duckie? Oh! by the way, Godden's the name, Bill Godden.'

After that, for the next two weeks or more, he was in the *café* every night. The embarrassment of a nightly tray of strawberries left on the threshold of the house provided her with a dilemma she found hard to solve. A mask of coldness seemed the only answer and it was a great mistake.

It took Godden, cocky, inquisitive, quick-mouthed, a mere night or two to size up Brady as the figure of fun.

Over infinite plates of egg-and-chips and endless cups of tea he was the lead in a nightly game of banter.

'Ever heard of that song, Jim boy?'

'What song was that, Bill?'

' "*Billikins and His Dinah*".'

'Can't say as I ever did.'

'No? Don't know how it goes?'

'Can't say I do.'

' "*With a cup o' cold p'ison laid down by her side*".'

'No. Can't say I ever heard of it, Bill. I heard of *Nancy kittle me fancy*, though.'

'Kittle, eh? I'll lay it's a kittle too. Like a fly settling on a mare.'

There was always much laughter in the *café*.

At first all this went on behind her back. She remained as blissfully unaware of it as she was deluded into the belief that her love for Brady was a secret no one else could possibly share.

Then one evening towards the end of September she made another mistake. The sight of Godden unloading yet another tray of strawberries from his three-tonner and carrying it across the concrete apron towards the house was suddenly too much for her nerves, tired and ragged already from a long, rushed day in the *café*. She marched across the apron with lips tightened.

'I told you a million times already I don't want them. Take them back.'

'Last chance, duckie. Crop's finished. Last load tonight. More's the pity.'

'My heart'll break.'

'I'll be by every night, though. Cauliflowers from now on.'

'So now it's choke me with cauliflowers —'

He set the tray of strawberries down on the threshold of the house, as usual, and laughed in that cool, cocky way of his.

'Ah! come on. Be nice. I still fancy you.'

'Like I said, you'll fancy on.'

He laughed again, this time not so cockily but with the first hint of a sneer.

'Perhaps Lover boy'll be luckier.'

Riled, with lips tighter than ever, she said :

'And what was that supposed to mean?'

Again he laughed cockily.

'Now don't tell me you've never heard of Lover boy. I thought everybody knew about Lover boy.'

'I know dirt when I see it.'

'Everybody knows about Lover boy. Billikins. Don't tell me you don't know about Billikins.'

Again she somehow resisted the impulse to smack his face and frigidly, instead, started to walk away.

'The wild Irish boy,' Godden called after her. 'No? Not the wild Irish boy?'

This sudden betrayal of a situation she had so fondly imagined to be both precious and secret drove her, that night, in bed, closer than ever into Brady's arms. Pity for him increased and deepened her tenderness.

'I don't care for myself,' she told him. 'It's not for myself.'

'It's just how the fellers are.'

'I'll close the whole place down rather than –'

'I thought of taking a few days off in any case,' he suddenly said. 'I've been thinking I should go and see my sister.'

'Sister? What sister?'

'The one in Athlone. She's the eldest. I owe her money. I should have sent it months ago.'

'You can send it now. You don't have to go to her.'

'One of the lorry fellers promised me a lift as far as Manchester. It's only a flea hop from there to Liverpool.'

She drew him more closely down in the bed.

'You promised you wouldn't go away from me. You promised me a dozen times.'

'I'll not go away. I'll be back. This feller'll give me a lift back.'

'Don't go,' she said and again she found herself constricted between tears and laughter. 'Don't go, please. I can't bear it if you go.'

Two nights later, while she was still busy in the *café*, Brady slipped out, hitched his lift to Manchester and left without a word. It never once occurred to her that this abrupt departure of his might have been his way of saving her great distress. Until well past midnight she walked crazily about the place, calling his name. Sleeplessly, after that, she sat alone in the *café*, lights full on, making and drinking endless cups of tea, staring into empty space, brooding bitterly.

After a week had gone by, and then another, she began to be aware that whenever she walked into the *café* the air seemed to become charged with sudden tension, dangerously clenched. She had always treated every driver, with the exception of Godden, with equal friendliness. Now she found herself withdrawn from them, hostile, defensive, not speaking, at times unable even to pass the time of day. Soon this first withdrawal led to an even deeper one. She could no longer bear to be seen in public. Utterly reclusive, she began to keep to her room, leaving the running of the *café* to the two sisters from down the road. Gnawing at her own thoughts, not sleeping, she brooded alone.

The wind of winter began to whip in from the sea. Every day there were fewer lorries parked on the concrete apron. Presently one of the sisters got herself a job in a canning factory. The money was good, the hours were short and soon the other sister followed. Soon drivers began to arrive at the *café* to find no tea, no chips, no Francie and often no heating. The sign that Brady had earlier proudly painted and put up outside, saying *A HOT MEAL AT ANY HOUR* began to seem like a mere mockery of itself and on a day in December she took it down.

The next day she locked the *café*. Once again she was left with only services to offer : petrol, oil, and where was the nearest place you could get a decent cup of tea or coffee.

'Six gallons please, miss.' On a bitter January afternoon two men drew up in a jeep on the concrete apron. There was a touch of snow in the air. 'By God, it's cold. Open for tea?'

'Pardon?' Francie said.

'I said open for tea?'

No, she said, no. She didn't do teas now. That was a thing of the past.

She finished putting the six gallons into the tank of the jeep. The driver gave her two pound notes and she put them into her pocket. Bitter though the air was it seemed to her suddenly that she could smell the sea. In a flash she was thinking of a summer morning, a sea-poppy that was pale yellow, a sea-thistle blue as steel and four fresh herrings wrapped in newspaper.

'Forgotten something, haven't you, miss?'

'Pardon?'

'How about my change?'

Without a word she counted out the driver's change. The jeep started up. She watched it move, gather speed and finally vanish down the road.

A few thin sharp flakes of snow started to whip in from the direction of the sea. Unaware of them, she stood there for some long time afterwards, staring, eyes empty, alone in the middle of nowhere.

MORE ABOUT PENGUINS

Penguinews, which appears every month, contains details of all the new books issued by Penguins as they are published. From time to time it is supplemented by *Penguins in Print*, which is a complete list of all available books published by Penguins. (There are well over three thousand of these.)

A specimen copy of *Penguinews* will be sent to you free on request, and you can become a subscriber for the price of the postage. For a year's issues (including the complete lists) please send 30p if you live in the United Kingdom, or 60p if you live elsewhere. Just write to Dept EP, Penguin Books Ltd, Harmondsworth, Middlesex, enclosing a cheque or postal order, and your name will be added to the mailing list.

Note: *Penguinews* and *Penguins in Print* are not available in the U.S.A. or Canada

L. P. HARTLEY

THE GO-BETWEEN

'Of all the novels L. P. Hartley has written I think *The Go-Between* is the best ... It is in what is to me the best tradition of fiction' – John Betjeman in the *Daily Telegraph*

In one of the first and finest of the post-war studies of early adolescence, a boy of twelve describes a summer visit to a Norfolk country house at the beginning of the century. Not yet equipped to understand the behaviour of adults, he is guiltily involved in a tragic drama between three grown-up people. The author forcefully conveys the intensity of an emotional experience which breeds a lasting mistrust of life.

H. E. BATES

FAIR STOOD THE WIND FOR FRANCE

'*Fair Stood the Wind for France* is perhaps the finest novel of the war ... The scenes are exquisitely done and the characters – tenderly and beautifully drawn – are an epitome of all that is best in the youth of the two countries. This is a fine, lovely book which makes the heart beat with pride' – *Daily Telegraph*

DULCIMA

Dulcima is beautiful and determined ... Dulcima wants money ... and Dulcima is in terrible danger ...

THE WEDDING PARTY

A collection of thirteen short stories ranging from the humour of *The Picnic* and *Early One Morning* to the tragedy of *The Primrose Place* and the drama of sorrow and beauty of *The Wedding Party*.
Each one is a slice of life – your life.

A MOMENT IN TIME

She was still in her teens when they came to fight a war in the air. Day by precarious day she shared with these dedicated youngsters – hardly more than boys – dangers unbearably heightened by the peace of the English countryside.

THE DISTANT HORNS OF SUMMER

James's new nanny was seventeen years old and almost as innocent as he was. Life was good together. She entered into his imaginary world. She made friends with his invisible 'mates', Mr Pimm and Mr Monday. Then Mr Ainsworth came along. From the very beginning James's new nanny gave more attention to him. It was enough to make a boy leave home ...